VANILLA & VENDETTAS

FROSTED MISFORTUNES, BOOK 3

LISA SIEFERT

WHISKERED MYSTERIES

Cover Designer: Lou Harper at Cover Affairs
Logo Design: Mallory Rock at Rock Solid Book Designs
Editors: Jasmine Bryner, Megan Records, and Teri at the Editing Fairy
Proofreader: Jasmine Bryner

Whiskered Mysteries
PO Box 72
Brighton, MI 48116

Created with Vellum

ABOUT THIS BOOK

Hi. I'm Ava Decker and I own Frosted, the only stuffed cupcake bakery in all of Blueberry Bay. After being ghosted at the altar back in San Diego. I moved back home to Clover Creek, Maine, quit my boring accounting job, and turned my passion for pastries into a new career crafting the best stuffed cupcakes in the area. Along with becoming a pastry chef, I also became a kitty mom to an adorable ruddy Abyssinian cat, Lucky, who was raised by dogs as a kitten and now believes he is one. He can do everything a dog can do.

Fetch, check.

Tricks for treats, check.

Long walks outside, check.

Rolling over, check.

Licking my face to death, check.

Eating everything in sight, check.

But coming back when called, not so much.

I've never owned a pet in my life before Lucky but I'm told this is not normal feline behavior. Except for ignoring me when I call him. Apparently, that is totally normal cat behavior. But the rest was all canine-inherited from his doggy mommy he grew up with. Since he also suffers from separation anxiety, he's pretty much with me 24/7 so I had Frosted declared an official cat cafe and now everyone loves bringing their furry friends in.

He also accompanies me on murder investigations around town. It's not like I seek these types of activities out. I somehow always manage to stumble upon dead bodies surrounded by cupcakes. But this time, it's a valuable diamond ring that goes missing from the cupcake bakery. Why me?!

1

There is something so magical about surprise marriage proposals. Seeing the confused but happy look on someone's face, along with the tears of joy streaming down their cheeks. Oh, wait, those tears were streaming down *my* cheeks. I grabbed a tissue to wipe them away but Lucky, my adorable and faithful Abyssinian kitten, beat me to it. He pressed his little kitty paws against my face to blot out the tears, like they were tiny bugs to squash.

I was pretending to clean up Frosted's main cupcake display counter but secretly listening to Tyler and Shelby's date. The engagement ring was hidden inside the oversized cupcake that I just served to Shelby. I lied and told her it was a new jumbo cupcake size I wanted to try out. She was about to take her first bite, which would have been straight into a velvet ring box, enclosed inside a plastic baking bag for safety.

"Ouch! Oh, my stars! There's something hard inside this cupcake," she said, pulling it back to examine the source.

"There is?" asked Tyler, pretending to be surprised. "Let's see."

They both scraped frosting and cupcake crumbs back to reveal a box. Shelby tore open the plastic wrap, exposing the exquisitely crafted red velvet box inside with the signature Harry Wilson crest gold foiled on the top. Tyler had to special order it from London. It cost him an entire year's salary, making it the most compact representation of one hundred thousand dollars I'd ever seen when he dropped it off to me this morning to hide inside the cupcake.

"Should we tell Ava? Maybe she dropped this in here by accident," said Shelby, looking around the bakery for me. I instantly dived behind the counter to hide. How could she not know that was a surprise engagement ring? Or maybe she did and wondered if it was for someone else? Those things might have been going through my mind if I were to find an engagement ring since I was known for jumping to the wrong conclusion more than once.

"I think it's for you," said Tyler, placing a hand on Shelby's arm when she rose from her seat to return the box. Then he got down on one knee and popped the question that every woman in love is dying to hear from the man they're dating. "Shelby Hicks, will you make me the happiest man on Earth and marry me?"

It was Friday at Frosted, the one day of the week that we stayed open late. There were tons of other couples there, some college kids studying and a few people on their laptops. Once Tyler dropped to his knees, everyone stopped what they were doing and focused on the happy couple, particularly Shelby. We were all holding our breath while waiting to find out what her answer would be.

I knew Shelby would say yes. Since the minute I met her, the only thing she talked about was: *Tyler this, Tyler that, isn't Tyler so dreamy?* Plus, being incredibly superstitious, she believed everything was a sign of something bigger. If Tyler proposed, she'd take it as a sign they should get married.

"Ohmigosh, Tyler. Yes, yes, yes! I'll marry you," she said, leaping into his arms as he stood up to hug her.

The entire bakery, including myself, started to holler and applaud. It was the happiest Friday night ever at Frosted.

Shelby tore off the plastic protective covering on the velvet box and opened the top. We were all waiting for her to put on the ring and show it to everyone but instead, she crinkled her forehead and said, "That's odd. There's nothing in here."

"What do you mean, there's nothing in there?" asked Tyler, taking the box.

"It's empty," said Shelby. She looked around herself in case it might have dropped onto the ground.

They both started to look through the cupcake crumbs and frosting to see if it fell out somehow. I emerged from behind the counter to join them. Lucky followed me and hopped up onto the table, trying to figure out what we were all searching for with such intensity.

"Are you sure it didn't fall into the box somehow?" I asked, pointing to the red velvet box and hoping there was some sort of secret lining area.

We all took turns feeling the box.

"You're sure this is the right cupcake?" asked Tyler, looking panicked.

"Yes, of course, it's the right cupcake," I said. Why would I deliberately put a red velvet box in someone else's cupcake? And this was a cupcake shop, not a jewelry store. We didn't have any other red velvet boxes lying around. "As soon as you gave it to me this morning, I locked it up in the safe all day until you texted me that you were on your way. Then I took it out and popped it into this cupcake." I pointed to the table crumbs.

Tyler and I planned it all out this morning to the last detail when he dropped off the ring. He texted me as they were leaving dinner so I'd be ready. I saved them their favorite booth and made sure to serve them myself. I even gave the rest of the staff the entire day off so there wouldn't be any confusion or accidental servings of the wrong cupcake.

"So where is it?" asked Tyler, looking at me with a definite tone of accusation in his voice.

Lucky started pushing things off the counter, the crumbs, the fork, and finally, the red velvet box. "Not helping, Lucky," I said, picking him up.

2

After everyone gave their statements to the police, I handed each person a free cupcake voucher on their way out. I hated thinking that their most recent memory would be a cupcake shop that ruined love and stole diamond engagement rings.

"Decker, how do you always manage to be at the epicenter of every major crime in Clover Creek?" asked Wesley. He was stepping into Frosted, along with the crime scene investigation team. Wesley was the only detective in all of Clover Creek and someone I kept running into, despite my sincere efforts to lead a completely innocent and non-criminal baker's life.

When we first met, I thought I detected a romantic spark between the two of us but soon discovered that Wesley had a type, which was the polar opposite of pretty much everything about me. He preferred petite, stick-thin, blonde, blue-eyed women. At five-foot-eleven, no one ever described me as *petite* and my love of carbs prevented me from landing into the stick-thin category. Wesley's women were more like the Marilyn Monroe types when it came to beauty, whereas my fuzzy, brown hair and matching colored eyes simply relegated me to blending into the background. But Wesley was still one of the good guys and a close friend.

I shrugged my shoulders. "I guess I'm just lucky that way. I'd expect you to be happy it wasn't a dead body I stumbled upon." Since returning home to Clover Creek from San Diego back in January, I found not one, not two, but *three* dead bodies in the last four months. Although I had nothing to do with anyone's demise, my discoveries instantly made me look guilty. Was it my fault that I always seemed to be in the wrong place at the wrong time?

Lucky thought I was calling him when I said I was *lucky* and he hopped over. He climbed up my leg and nestled into my arms where I hugged him and gave him a little kitty kiss. "Good boy," I said, placing him in his tiny kitty bjorn on my chest. That was his favorite place to be. It was great during the winter and colder spring days but now that we were well into June, the summer heat and humidity were settling in, and having a kitty heater on my chest wasn't quite as enjoyable as it previously was. I made a mental note to look into kitty-friendly purses he could fit into instead.

I walked Wesley through my entire day after receiving the ring until it came up missing. He listened intently and took copious notes.

"Who else knows the combination to the safe?" he asked, flipping his notepad to a new page.

"Besides me, only Ruby but she would never steal a diamond ring and even if she wanted to, she's been in Boston all week at an insurance conference," I said. Ruby was my best friend and silent partner. She was CEO of her family business, Hardison Insurance, whose office was down the street. Neither one of us had opened the safe since I inherited Frosted from its previous owner, Francine. Francine's brother, Grant, installed the safe a week before Francine died and considering Grant was now sitting in a jail cell, serving a life sentence for killing Francine, it was highly unlikely he could have taken it either.

"Grant's still in prison, right?" I asked Wesley just to be sure. Weirder things were known to happen.

"As far as I know. Why?" replied Wesley, pausing his blue ballpoint pen in midair while awaiting my answer.

"He's the one that bought the safe for Francine. He probably knows the combination to open it," I said, giving Lucky a small scratch behind his ears while he purred.

I never understood why he bought her a safe. There weren't many valuables to hide from prying eyes in a cupcake bakery. Tyler's engagement ring was the first time I ever had the need to use it.

"I seriously doubt Grant broke out of a supermax prison like Statesville and swiftly beelined it here to steal an engagement ring that he had no idea about; but I'll double-check that right after I verify Ruby's alibi. In the meantime, I noticed your back door was unlocked. Did you forget to secure it from a delivery earlier or when you came in this morning to open the bakery?" asked Wesley, pointing to the back room.

"I always leave the back door unlocked for deliveries. I've never had a problem before," I said. I peeked over Wesley's shoulder toward that area.

"We'll need access to all the security camera footage," he said. He pointed his pen toward the cameras and sensors installed throughout the bakery.

"What footage?" I asked. I gathered a dozen cupcakes from the fridge and placed them on a serving tray.

"Didn't my niece, Chloe, set up a state-of-the-art security system for you that sits on a cloud so it can't be manually erased?" he asked.

"You mean that super pricey system that I stopped paying the monthly bills on to save money and as a result, they shut it off?" I asked. Frosted was barely breaking even and I still had a mountain of wedding debt to pay off from the San Diego wedding that never happened. Despite the fact that the groom was a no-show, the credit card companies still wanted their money and while slightly sympathetic, none of them were interested in providing refunds.

Wesley sighed and put his head in his hands. "Decker," he said with a more than obvious hint of disappointment. While I called him by his first name, he preferred to call me by my last name and not in that sweet, endearing, male-bonding way. More in the *what-have-you- done-now?!* way.

I placed the huge tray of cupcakes onto one of the tables in the middle of the main room and announced to everyone, "Who wants cupcakes? These are on the house."

Between the original officers that responded to the call and the crime scene team, almost a dozen cops were gathered in the room, which pretty much totaled the entire Clover Creek Police Department. There wasn't a whole lot of crime in town, if any, so everyone who was anyone on the police force was down here.

"Hmm. I wonder why you're not making enough to pay your bills?" asked Wesley. "Isn't your boyfriend a billionaire? Can't you just borrow some money from him?"

"Marcus is not my boyfriend," I replied. Why did everyone keep saying that? Not that I wouldn't mind dating Marcus but his interest seemed purely platonic. He enjoyed solving mysteries with me and sharing a slice of deep dish pizza but beyond that, the closest we ever got was when his hand accidentally brushed mine while analyzing the murder board together. I wouldn't exactly classify that as a budding romance.

"Could've fooled me by the way he looks at you," said Wesley. He held up his palm to block me when I tried to offer him a cupcake.

"Don't be ridiculous. He looks at me like anyone else does," I said. I wanted to believe Wesley but Marcus hadn't made a single move on me beyond simply being extra friendly. That was only because I was helping him figure out who murdered one of the contestants in his beauty pageant. He had a business stake in finding the killer.

"Trust me. I'm a guy and I only look at my girlfriend or a girl I'm interested in like that," said Wesley.

Was I starting to blush? I kind of wished it were true but I felt silly saying it out loud or even acknowledging Wesley's statement in any way.

"I can make you a spirulina smoothie if you want. Everything's ready to go in the back." I said, changing the subject. There was no use speculating over my inactive love life.

I would rather starve than choke a spirulina smoothie down but Ruby was a committed fan to having at least one if not more every day so there was always a Vitamix blender and fresh ingredients set up in the back for when she visited. Since she was currently in Boston, no one had touched it but Wesley was a big health nut and I knew he loved them.

"Yes, that would be great. I'll come with you and take another look at the safe," he said, following me to the back.

Lucky bounced out of his kitty bjorn and ran ahead of us when I pointed the way for Wesley. Technically, only employees were allowed to go there but the shop was closed and my assistant always cleaned everything in the morning before prepping cupcakes for the day. Plus, with all the crime scene investigators traipsing through here, I'd have to do an extra deep clean tonight anyway.

The back room of Frosted was actually pretty spacious. Frosted used to be a quick-serve, old-fashioned diner in another life. The peek-through window from the front to the back was designed to pass the food orders directly from the kitchen. I left the huge peek-through hole open and decorated it instead of filling it in. It gave the bakery some character and I think people liked to catch glimpses of the big dough mixers and ovens. It helped add more authenticity to my claim that everything was made from scratch on-site.

Experimenting to create new stuffed cupcake creations was my favorite pastime. I tried to add three new flavors each month and June's specials were the Pumpkin Spiced Caramel Cupcakes, the Strawberry Filled Tiramisu Cupcakes with Mascarpone Buttercream Frosting, and the French Vanilla Cheesecake Filled Cupcakes.

While I started pulling spirulina smoothie ingredients out of the fridge, Lucky did little somersaults with his favorite red fuzzy ball before following Wesley around. He sniffed his pant cuffs and shoes a few times while tugging on them with this mouth.

"Your cat is so weird," said Wesley. He tried to gently shake him off.

"He wants you to play with him," I said. I tossed Lucky's fuzzy red ball towards Wesley. "Just throw it. He likes to play fetch."

Wesley easily caught the ball with one hand. "Does he know he's a cat and not a dog?" asked Wesley, tossing the ball across the room. Lucky leapt after it, dodging the mixer, hopping over the boxes, and finally retrieving the ball. He pranced back towards Wesley and dropped it at his feet.

"He may look like a cat on the outside but he's totally a dog on the inside," I said, setting aside the chopped celery and reaching into the fridge for some spinach.

"How did you end up with such a strange pet?" he asked.

"Seriously?" I replied. "You gave him to me."

Every time Wesley saw Lucky, I had to remind him where the cat came from. Perhaps he had anti-pet radar around him, making him forget everything about pets the minute they were out of sight. Lucky belonged to the former owner of Frosted from whom I inherited both the bakery and her house. I simply assumed Lucky was included in the estate. That, and Wesley tricked me into taking him by threatening to leave him with Animal Control where he'd be destroyed.

"Oops," said Wesley, after throwing the ball towards the back of the store before it sailed out the window and into the alley. Lucky did a huge kitty leap and pulled down the back door handle to open it, jumping into the alley and running after the ball. Wesley did a double-take and stared back at me, unsure if he really saw a cat open a door.

"He just learned how to open doors," I said, remembering that I still needed to pick up some childproof door locks. The door handles were big, perpendicular letter L's, which Lucky easily clicked open with a single tug. I was actually pretty impressed that he caught on so quickly.

Wesley and I both went out after him.

"Lucky, come back!" I called, hoping there were no cars out there. The ball bounced off the back fence on the other side of the alley and rolled into the shop next door. Kira owned the flower shop there and was probably working late on an early morning delivery. She loved Lucky so hopefully, she wouldn't mind the uninvited intrusion into her shop before I could stop him.

We both raced inside Gorgeous Greens. Lucky trotted around like he owned the place, finding his little red kitty ball and turning back before dropping it at Wesley's feet.

"Good boy," said Wesley, picking up the ball. He was about to throw it again when I stopped him.

I opened my palm for the ball, signaling for Wesley to put it into my hand. "I think that's enough fetch for one night."

"Hi, Ava," said Kira, coming out from her huge flower refrigerator. She pulled off her shearing gloves and fanned out her hair, which was pointless. Kira looked absolutely flawless every time I saw her. Her cascading silky, blonde hair made her look more like a modern-day Cinderella than a florist. "Have you been here long? I didn't even hear you come in. I'm trying to get a big order ready for tomorrow."

"Sorry to barge in like this but Lucky's ball rolled in here and we were chasing him," I said, trying to hunt him down. He was in his kitty heaven, sniffing one plant, then another.

I caught Lucky midstream. He switched from just sniffing the plants to digging them up and swiftly finished emptying a potted fern before moving on to a potted cactus. He yowled in anger at being stopped but I held strong. I didn't want him ruining *all* of her inventory.

"I'm so sorry about that. I'll clean it up," I said, looking around for a broom.

I tucked Lucky into his kitty bjorn and found a broom and dustpan hanging on the back wall next to some old men's clothes.

"Don't worry about that. Who would Lucky be if he wasn't distracting you every minute of every day? Now who is this *we* you're referring to?" she asked, looking from me to Wesley.

"Sorry. Kira, this is Detective Wesley Lockwood.

Wesley, this is my neighbor, Kira, who owns Gorgeous Greens," I said. Considering they'd never met before, I quickly assumed Wesley wasn't the flower giving type of boyfriend. I made a mental note to advise Wesley to buy his girlfriend some flowers once in a while. It couldn't hurt.

I finished scooping up the soil, dropped it into the waste bin, and hung the broom and dustpan back up in the corner.

"I'm also the star of the Clover Creek Community Playhouse production of *Much Ado About Nothing,*" she said, striking a dramatic pose. "I just got promoted to the lead female role."

"Wow, that's fantastic," I said, running up and giving her a congratulatory hug. "But I thought my baking assistant, Caitlin, was playing the lead?"

"Yes, until Caitlin got a summer scholarship; between the condensed course schedule and working at Frosted, she won't have time to do that and still be in the play," said Kira with a wink.

"Let me guess, the scholarship was provided by Gorgeous Greens?" I asked, pulling up a seat at one of Kira's flower arrangement stations while keeping Lucky on my lap so I could supervise him.

"I have no idea what you're talking about," said Kira. She put on her most devious smile, batted her eyelashes, and pretended to look confused.

"Congratulations on your stardom but you really shouldn't leave your back door unlocked," said Wesley, inspecting her door locks. "There was a diamond theft next door."

"Aren't you a knight in shining armor? Do you always help out local damsels in distress?" asked Kira, hopping closer to Wesley and looping her arms through his.

"He is a knight to his girlfriend," I said, pulling Kira

away from Wesley, who quickly moved back to the door, pretending to inspect it to avoid Kira.

Kira leaned in and whispered, "Until a man is married, he's fair game."

"I'm not sure if it works that way," I said. I guessed Kira never heard of the girl code. "Isn't that what broke up you and Tyler?"

Wesley's ears perked up at hearing that and he stopped fiddling with her door. "You were dating Tyler?"

"Yeah, like over a decade ago. That's ancient history," said Kira, leaning against the flower arrangement table.

Wesley pulled out his blue ballpoint pen and started writing down some notes. "Were you at Frosted today and did you have access to the ring?" he asked.

"Yes and yes but I didn't steal it," she said. "I was in rehearsals pretty much all day today, which is why I'm working so late tonight."

"I can vouch for her. She was in at the same time as Tyler this morning when he dropped off the ring. I was helping her by sewing some sequins into her costume," I said. I wasn't an expert seamstress or anything but I knew how to sew on buttons and hem pants.

"Speaking of which, can you hem those pants for me, the ones hanging up on the hook?" she asked.

"Sure, but maybe later tomorrow?" I replied to which she gave me a thumbs-up.

Wesley cleared his throat to cut off our conversation. "So you wouldn't mind if I looked around?" he asked, already rifling through the flower pots and soil buckets.

Kira extended her arms out and said, "Be my guest. You can even get the CSI tech team in here to test me for traces of diamond dust."

"Diamonds are not guns. They don't leave diamond dust

residue like gunpowder does," said Wesley, who was completely clueless to Kira's flirting attempts.

Thirty minutes later, both Wesley and the Clover Creek tech team searched all of Gorgeous Greens and came up empty. I spent that time helping Kira prep her flowers for the next day.

Mouthing the word *sorry* to Kira as we all left so she could close up for the night, I set Lucky down once I saw the alleyway was empty.

Wesley followed us back into Frosted.

"You should still lock this back door," he said.

"It's Clover Creek. It's so safe here, there's never a problem," I said, washing my hands in the sink.

"And diamond engagement rings never go mysteriously missing?" he asked, pulling off his gloves and dropping them in the recycle bin.

"Touché. But until today, nothing bad ever happened here," I said. I grew up here. It was the safest place in the world. Everybody knew everyone else or someone who did.

"Wasn't the owner of Frosted killed inside her own cupcake truck?" he asked. That was how we met. Wesley pulled me over for speeding in the Frosted cupcake truck and when he opened the back, we discovered Francine's dead body.

"Yeah, by her half-brother. Considering I'm an only child, I consider myself safe," I said.

"Have you seen any more dead bodies in the cupcake truck? Or have any other diamonds gone missing?" I asked.

Even though I realized my arguments were pointless and borderline silly, being around Wesley always put me on the defensive. I was terrible at debate so nonsensical babble usually came out whenever I attempted to do so but he should have been used to it by now.

If Wesley wasn't arresting me for a crime I didn't commit or accusing me of something I hadn't done, he was usually chastising me for investigating his open murder cases or warning me to stay out of them. But if not for me, the last two homicides in Clover Creek, that of Frosted's previous owner and Wesley's ex-girlfriend, would've remained unsolved. You'd think I deserved to get a medal or some sort of commendation but no! All I got was a big *stay out of it* warning.

"All I'm saying is you should keep your doors locked just to be safe and maybe even consider reactivating your security system," he said. On the plus side, there was nothing of value inside Frosted to steal. The industrial sized dough mixer was probably the highest ticket item in the place, which weighed almost half a ton and was securely bolted to the ground. Those weren't too high in demand, last time I checked and even if they were, good luck trying to steal it.

While I tossed the rest of his spirulina smoothie ingredients into the Vitamixer, Wesley locked and bolted the back door shut. "See? How hard was that to do?"

It wasn't difficult at all but it also made receiving supply deliveries so much easier if your vendors could come and go at will. No need to coordinate schedules.

"And remember, no investigating this on your own," he said, wagging a finger at me for emphasis.

"You know I only do those sorts of things with Ruby and she's out of town until Monday," I said.

"Well, I'm back early. Didn't you get my text?" Ruby asked, coming in from the front. Lucky ran over to greet her by doing his usual kitty crawl up her pant legs and climbing into her open arms. She hugged him and bounced over to the counter, picking up Wesley's drink and gulping it down. "Spirulina smoothie!"

3

"Wakey, wakey!" chimed Ruby as she opened my bedroom door.

If I played dead and ignored her, would she go away?

It was nine AM, which was usually the time I started thinking about getting up, not physically doing it but simply pondering the possibility of doing so. Ruby had already finished her morning jog, showered, and cleaned the entire house, judging by the background noises I heard while sleeping in. She skipped over to the drapes and mercilessly swung them open, flooding the room with summer sunshine.

I pulled the covers over my head. "How are you so cheerful and buoyant at nine AM? Shouldn't you be suffering from jetlag or something?" I asked. We both scoured every inch of Frosted after Wesley left in the vain hope of finding the missing diamond engagement ring. It was well after midnight by the time we got back home and went to bed.

"It's only a four-hour flight to Boston, which is in the same time zone as Clover Creek, and I did some light calisthenics in the plane so I'm fully refreshed and ready to make a grocery store run with you," she said, flinging back the covers.

This time, it was Lucky's turn to groan. He was definitely not a morning kitty. Blissfully snoring away while draped across my neck like a kitty sweater, he was in his favorite sleeping spot. It was super cute and comforting during the colder winter months but it was mid-June, and over ninety degrees already. Sleeping at night with him now felt like I was in a sauna. For a tiny, four-pound Abyssinian kitten, he radiated a lot of body heat. I slowly slid him onto his own pillow to free myself.

"Why do we need to go to the grocery store?" I asked Ruby, now that I was more awake and my brain began to function somewhat clearer. The eager determination in her voice made me think there was an actual emergency or something.

"You're out of spirulina smoothie ingredients! What am I going to have for breakfast?" she asked, rolling up the vacuum cleaner cord and storing it in the closet, which held her second wardrobe. When I inherited the house from my former boss, I also received all of her clothes. They fit Ruby perfectly at five-foot-four and were way too tiny for me at five-foot-eleven. It was super convenient for times like this when the airline lost her luggage or she spent the night for sleepovers.

"It's been like twelve hours since your last one. We might need to consider putting you into a spirulina smoothie addiction program," I said, half-joking, half-wishing a facility like that really existed so I could secretly drop her off there.

"You love my spirulina smoothies," said Ruby, looking confused at the thought that anyone could resist them.

"I do," I said with as much glee as I could muster. Just

thinking about the sour, bitter aftertaste made me nearly gag. Unfortunately, they were Ruby's culinary pride and joy and saying anything to the contrary would have hurt her feelings, so I kept up the ruse that I loved them just as much as she did.

"Great, let's go," she said, pulling me by the arm out of bed. "We can take that fancy sports car sitting in the garage. I found the keys in this summer dress in the closet," she said, swinging a silver key fob around her finger.

"You know that car has no insurance, no registration, and probably, no gas," I said, yawning and reaching my arms out to stretch myself awake. "Plus, neither of us knows how to drive stick-shift. Not to mention the fact that it's probably stolen."

"Well, someone's a Negative Nancy this morning. Aren't you the least bit amazed that I found the keys to your mystery car?" she asked, continuing to dangle the keys in front of me.

"Isn't it more amazing that your dress has pockets?" I asked. I'd give anything to have more dresses with pockets. Why didn't all dresses feature pockets? There should be a place where you could send any dress in the world to have pockets sewn on for you. It would be the best service ever. Men always have pockets in pants. The world was so unfair.

"Fine. We can take your car," she said, placing the silver fob on the bedside table.

Her dress rang. It was her cell phone, safely hidden in her other dress pocket and coincidentally proving my point on how convenient dress pockets were.

"Maybe it's the airport calling because they found my luggage," she said, pulling it out.

She saw the caller ID and slumped herself down on the

edge of the bed. "Oh, hey, Dad," she said, putting him on speaker.

"What kind of a greeting is that for your favorite dad in the whole world?" he asked, pretending to be hurt.

"Sorry. I thought you were the airlines calling with my lost luggage," she said. "And of course, you're my favorite dad. You're my only dad."

"Hi, Mr. Hardison," I chimed in. "You're my second favorite dad in the whole world. Does that help?"

"Ava! How is my favorite pastry chef doing?" he asked.

"I'm starving. Any chance of you making your award-winning Pancake Towers for breakfast?" I asked, crossing my fingers and holding my breath. It could totally get me out of spirulina smoothie ingredient shopping, which ran a close second only to my other least favorite activity: drinking said smoothies.

"That depends. Do you prefer Oreo Cookie or Double Chocolate Brownie Batter Pancakes?" he asked.

"Both," answered Ruby and I at the same time.

I leaped out of bed and bounced up and down, doing my version of a pancake happy dance. Then I jumped into the shower and got ready in record time.

Lucky was still sleeping when I came out so I carefully placed him into his kitty carrier before we all headed to Pancake Tower Central, also known as Ruby's parents' house.

Ruby's parents' house was only a fifteen minute drive from my place but the construction on Main Street turned it into a half-hour road trip.

"Sounds like someone finally woke up," said Ruby, turning the volume down on the radio.

There were some confused kitty meows coming from the back seat. "Good morning, little man," I chirped to him. My greeting was answered by some angry kitty scratching and growling. Lucky liked to stretch out when he woke up, but for kitty safety purposes, he was no longer allowed to ride in anything but his kitty carrier, which was securely anchored to the backseat.

"Whoa. Someone is not a morning kitty," said Ruby, changing her direction on the radio volume from low to high.

I pointed towards the glove box. "There are some kitty treats in there that should tide him over until we get to your parents' house," I said. At least, I hoped there were. My satellite radio subscription to the Baby Mozart channel had expired due to lack of funds so I had nothing else to calm him with.

Traffic in Clover Creek was practically unheard of until the town voted to launch a new underground trolley system, which was causing a ton of havoc on the current roads. It was the biggest project since the Town Square Fountain was installed almost twenty years ago. The goal was to help people get around town during blizzards and dangerous winter white-out conditions, but it also had an ecological benefit of helping to eliminate emissions. I was fully behind it except during times like this when it was all that stood between me and Oreo Cookie Pancake Towers.

The cement truck blocking traffic finally moved. I hit the gas but instead of going forward, the car lurched ahead in a big jump as smoke streamed out from under the front hood before it made a sad, screeching sound and just died.

"What was that?" asked Ruby, swiveling her body towards the front again. Lucky meowed at the sudden stoppage of steady kitty treats into his carrier. "Why is there smoke coming out of your car?"

"Maybe it overheated?" I guessed. We both hopped out of the car and ran over to the front to inspect it, which was actually kind of silly. Alone, neither of us knew the first thing about car repair or maintenance, and together, we probably knew even less.

"Do you think it's going to explode?" asked Ruby, slowly backing away from the engine. "That's what happens on TV."

It seemed highly unlikely. But just in case, I doubled back to the car and extricated Lucky from the back seat.

"We should've taken the sports car," said Ruby.

Before I could remind her again of everything wrong with that suggestion, her phone dinged. She held it up. It was a photo text from her dad of our Pancake Towers. They were as tall as the Eiffel Tower and drizzled with *Nutella*.

I thought I heard whimpering from Lucky but it was me. I was the one doing all the whimpering.

4

An hour later, the AAA guy pulled up and helped us maneuver the car to the shoulder of the road so traffic could pass by more easily. If he could hurry it up, there was still enough time to make it to Ruby's parents' house before our pancakes got cold. I could already taste the divine, sugary nectar melting in my mouth. He inspected the car and leaned out the driver's side seat as he signaled for me to come over.

"When was the last time you changed the oil?" he asked.

"Oil?" I repeated, jolting myself out of my Pancake Tower daydreams. *Oil?* Why was he asking me about oil? I had no idea. This wasn't even my car.

"You do know that you need to change the oil every six months or five thousand miles, right?" he asked, hopping out. He pulled a switch under the dash that opened the front hood, which was still steaming.

Ugh. I did an instant faceplant on my palm. My dad would so kill me when he returned. That was the one thing that he kept telling me to do before taking off on his cruise a couple months ago. It was so expensive that I put it on the list to do later and then I just forgot about it. I mean, how much driving could there be in a small town like Clover Creek? I was only a couple thousand miles over the suggested limit. I guessed it all added up over time.

"I vaguely recall someone telling me about getting oil changes," I said, wishing for a time machine. I peered over the engine that was more visible now that the steam cleared away.

"It looks like your car is completely out of oil," he said, pulling out the dipstick, to which a tiny drop of black clung to the end.

"Shouldn't the car have alerted me that it's overdue for an oil change?" I asked, popping back into the driver's seat to grab my purse from the passenger seat. My Palmer Tech SmartWatch gave me alerts all the time. Eat more veggies, have a piece of fruit, walk more often, stop sitting so long, blah blah blah. Couldn't a car with electronic gadgets built into it tell me when it needed a quart of oil?

"You mean, like the oil gauge here, which is currently hovering over the red danger alert section?" he asked, following me over to the driver's side. He leaned in and pointed to the dial on the dashboard.

"Oh, so that's what that's for," I said. Who had time to check out every single gauge on their car? There were so many. You had the radio, the GPS navigation system, the speedometer, the accelerometer, the temperature gauge, the turn signals, the climate control system, the lights...

It was a good thing my parents were out of town on yet another cruise. This was the second time I had to call AAA for a tow since I borrowed their car. Hopefully, I could get it fixed before they returned. I'd never hear the end of it if I failed.

"Hey, weren't you the same person who called last

month after driving this same car into a potato field?" he asked.

"Maybe. But I'm sure lots of people accidentally drive into potato fields all the time. It's Maine. They're everywhere," I replied. All right, it was definitely me but it wasn't like I did it on purpose.

"I topped off your oil so it will drive now but stay off the highways and don't push it past forty until you get it looked at," he said. "Maybe try Clover Creek Collision and Auto Repair. Do you want me to write that down for you?"

"Thanks but I know where it is," I said since it was the only car repair shop in town.

He tore out the bottom page underneath the carbon copy on his clipboard and handed it to me. "Here's your receipt," he said. "Remember. In town driving only and don't push it past forty miles per hour."

"Got it. Stay under forty," I said, taking the receipt from him.

I folded it up and threw it into my purse. Even only going forty miles per hour, we could still make it to Ruby's parents' house in the next five minutes. "Are we ready?" I asked.

Ruby's phone dinged again and she held it up. It was her dad letting us know that our pancakes had gotten cold and he had to throw them out. Would it be weird to cry over spoiled pancakes?

"But can't he make another batch?" I whined in a cracked voice.

"He's meeting friends to go fishing for the day," she said. "The boat leaves the dock in a few minutes."

"No chance he wants to be a little late to that?" I asked. "You know how you Hardisons like to exercise. He could swim out to the boat."

"Don't worry. We're right in front of the Stop-N-Shop.

I'll just grab some spirulina smoothie ingredients for breakfast and we can walk over to Frosted to make them," she said, skipping off towards the store happily. Lucky followed her in. "I know you're starving so I'll be sure to get enough to make you a double."

"Oh, goody," I said, trying to hold back my tears and suppress my gag reflex.

Before I had a chance to be sad, my phone dinged. It was my dad.

Dad: *Just got a ping from AAA. Is everything okay? You remembered to change the oil, right?*

Me: *There is new oil in the car right now.*

Technically, that was true.

5

After carefully deflecting my dad's car maintenance questions and choking down a few sips of the extra-large spirulina smoothie Ruby made me, I doubled down and took a closer look through Frosted for the missing diamond ring. Even though the entire police force, Ruby, and myself had already combed every inch of this place last night, I started again from scratch.

"You really think you could magically drop a one hundred thousand dollar ring out of its sealed plastic bag while stuffing it into a cupcake?" asked Ruby.

I came out of the walk-in fridge after hiding the remains of my spirulina smoothie behind some cake boxes in the back. I shrugged and said, "Possibly. That ring didn't just evaporate into thin air. It has to be somewhere."

Ruby tossed back the rest of her smoothie and placed the cup in the dishwasher. "All right, I'll help you look again."

She headed towards the walk-in fridge but I jumped in front of her and cut her off. "We can skip that. It's definitely not in there."

"But I thought you wanted to double-check everything again?" she asked. She reached around me for the fridge door.

"Yes, double-check, not triple check. Let's divide and conquer the bakery. I'll do the back and you do the front," I said, gently turning her around and directing her towards the front of the shop. "We'll finish in half the time and then we can take off for the airport and see if they found your missing luggage."

Ruby seemed to ponder that over before she agreed. "Okay," she said, heading to the front door.

Unlike murder scenes, missing items didn't really have a crime scene so my baking assistant, Caitlin, was able to open Frosted today without the yellow caution tape or usual limitations. In homicides, the entire location is shut down until the murder is solved. If it could have helped us find the missing diamond ring sooner, I would gladly have done so.

Three hours later, my knees were killing me after crawling from one end of the bakery to the other on all fours. Lucky was having the greatest time ever. He hopped on top of me, did kitty somersaults underneath me and seemed to think we were playing leapfrog across the bakery. On the plus side, I did a thorough cleaning as I made my way through the bakery. Even though my search did not turn up the missing diamond, Frosted's interior was now sparkling and immaculate.

There was nothing left to do but head over to Shelby's and beg her to forgive me. She didn't seem in the least bit angry or annoyed last night, which only made me feel worse. The last time the diamond was seen was in my possession. It was really up to me to recover it and solve the case. No one wanted to find that diamond more than I did.

I helped Caitlin load all of today's cupcakes into the

display case as the barista was arriving. I let them know I was heading out for the day and asked if they could close up for me. On Saturdays, we were only open from noon to five so it was a short day. They were happy to get the extra hours and I was happy to get more time to investigate.

"We'll do a quick check-in on Shelby and then head out to the airport," I said to Ruby as we piled back into my parents' SUV.

Or rather, as I piled in. Ruby hesitated outside the passenger door. "Are you sure we should be driving this all the way to Bangor?" she asked. It was only an hour away and daytime. Worst case scenario, I'd have to call AAA again.

"We could always take your car," I replied. Ruby's place was only a few minutes' drive from Town Square. She recently bought one of those fancy electric cars that went super fast.

"We could if I had the keys but they're safely locked away in my lost luggage," she said.

"I don't understand why you put your car keys in your checked-in luggage?" I said. I started up the car. It made a pained, sputtering sound before slowly chugging to life.

"I was only trying to make my purse as light as possible and it's not like I needed them for the flight," she explained. "Why don't we call your boyfriend, Marcus, and see if he'll give us a ride or loan us his driver?"

"He's not my boyfriend and he's on a flight heading back here right now from Silicon Valley. He doesn't get in until later this afternoon," I replied.

"He could be your boyfriend if you did something other than investigating murders all the time," said Ruby.

"C'mon, are you getting in? Let's go," I said, wondering why Ruby was still hovering outside the car.

She backed away from the car. "I'm going to call the

airlines and ask if they will deliver my missing suitcase to my house when they find it."

"Don't you at least want me to drop you off at home?" I asked, buckling myself in.

"No, I'm good. I can walk from here. In fact, you should probably drive this straight to the car repair shop and then get a rideshare home," she said.

As if! I had a missing diamond engagement ring to locate. And a car filled with *I'm sorry I lost your ring* cupcakes that I had to deliver to Shelby at the library.

6

Clover Creek Library, where Shelby worked as an Assistant Librarian, was only a fifteen-minute drive from Town Square, where the bakery was. However, my newly capped speed limit of forty miles per hour made it more like a thirty-minute trip.

I hadn't been to the library since high school. Not because I didn't love books but because I was now an eReader-only girl. Why lug around one heavy book in your purse when your ten-ounce eReader could hold ten thousand books?

The library was situated right inside Maine's National Park and surrounded by lush forest land and nature. It could easily be mistaken for an extra-large log cabin. Although it was modern and new on the inside, the exterior still held that same *Little House on the Prairie* charm as it originally had when it was built in the early nineteen hundreds. I breathed in the fresh mountain air of pinecones, maple sap, and summer heat before heading to the library.

I set Lucky down once we were indoors and safely out of the tick danger zone. He hopped up onto the counter and immediately started nuzzling Shelby. He really liked her. She was one of his favorite people.

"Aww. It's my cute, little kitty angel, Lucky," she said, picking him up and giving him kisses. Shelby loved cats just as much as I did.

"I see your monthly allergy shots are still working," I said. Shelby was super allergic to cats but had started getting shots in anticipation of getting her own little kitten..

"Looks like it," she said, encircling her arms around Lucky in a sweet kitty embrace. "Natalia called yesterday and said she might have a little Lucky for me to pick up today. I'm hurrying to finish work so I can leave early in case she calls. I was late the last time and she sold the kitten to someone else so I don't want to miss out again."

Shelby was on the waiting list that Natalia, Lucky's breeder, kept for potential owners who were eager to adopt a little Abyssinian kitten of their own. Abyssinians had tiny litters since they tended to be considerably smaller in size, so waiting for one could take months if not years.

"That's exciting. Let's have a toast with this Mexican Mocha Latte I brought you, along with some of my new French Vanilla Cheesecake Filled Cupcakes with Sprinkles," I said, placing the container on the counter in front of Shelby.

"Ahh, my old friend, caffeine. You're my hero," said Shelby, coming behind the counter and hugging me. "This is perfect. I'm so tired. I was up all night with Madame Omega, my psychic, trying to figure out what the universe was telling me with the whole missing diamond ring incident," she said, releasing me and popping the lid off the latte. Taking a deep breath in, she smiled and added. "You're the best. How much do I owe you?"

"Nothing. I've been meaning to come over and visit you

in the library," I said, pretending to look around with an appreciative eye.

Not that it mattered. Shelby was totally focused on the food I brought her. She polished the cupcake off in two bites before washing it down with the latte.

"Whoa. That latte has a little kick to it. I like it! In all the craziness of last night, I didn't even get to have one of your amazing cupcakes," she said, reaching for a second one.

"About last night, I am so, so, very, very sorry about losing your engagement ring," I said; as if repeating words might give my apology more oomph. "That was all my fault."

"Don't be silly. Madame Omega said Mercury was in retrograde last night and my horoscope also foretold a disastrous event so I blame the universe, not you," she said. Reaching underneath the desk, she brought up a huge stack of books and tons of boxes of decorations. "Will you help me load this cart? I need to get all this stuff into the big conference room."

"Of course," I said, grabbing the books and carefully balancing the load onto the cart, while she pulled up more from under the desk. "What else did Madame Omega say?" I asked, hoping there was an upside to this.

Every time Shelby talked about her psychic, I had to resist doing a double eye roll. I found psychics just as fun and entertaining as the next person but never actually took them seriously. Especially for something as crucial as whom to spend the rest of your life with.

"Madame Omega thinks the stolen engagement ring was the universe telling me that I shouldn't marry Tyler," she said.

"Do you believe her?" I asked, hoping the answer was no.

"I don't know. Maybe," she said, looking down.

I made a mental note to personally visit this Debbie Downer Doomsday Psychic and set her straight onto the path of positivity or at the very least, closer to the path of neutrality. Instead of having Shelby hate me forever, Tyler would be the one to hate me forever if she turned down his proposal because of the missing diamond ring.

"Well, I have something that is totally going to cheer you up," I said, eager to change the subject. At least, until I could think of a better counterargument to her diehard belief in destiny, signs from the universe and karma.

"A mint chocolate chip ice cream sandwich from Claire's?" asked Shelby as we pushed the library cart over to the conference room.

This was why Shelby and I quickly became such good friends. She shared my love of Claire's Ice Cream Sandwiches. At first, we kept running into each other there by chance until we realized we both had a daily addiction to them.

"I'm going to find the missing ring for you," I said, pushing my weight into the library cart. These things were heavier than they looked once all the items were piled on.

"You are? But aren't the police already looking into it?" asked Shelby, dodging a tween who was walking and texting on their cell phone.

"Yes, but I've already successfully solved like, three different murders before the police did. Don't you want your ring found sooner rather than later?" I asked.

Shelby waved her hand in the air, dismissing my suggestion. "Not really. Tyler said the ring was fully insured with no deductible so you shouldn't waste any more time on it. He's not losing a penny over it. The insurance is cutting him a check sometime next week."

Duh. Of course, he had insurance. Who wouldn't insure

a ring that expensive? However, the fact remained that the proposal was still a bust. "But the police might still find the ring," I said.

"They said most stolen property is never recovered. When they found out Tyler insured it, they weren't overly concerned since no one got hurt," said Shelby. Lucky jumped up to the top of the book cart and scouted the library from his new higher vantage point.

What about my ego? That was pretty crushed. Someone from last night posted a video of the botched cupcake engagement debacle, naming me as the curse upon all things romance-related and Frosted as the place to go if you don't want a *happily ever after*. I had to figure out who really stole that ring if I wanted to redeem myself *and* my bakery.

"Just because the police have already given up doesn't mean we have to," I said. Not to mention how the guilt of losing that ring still gnawed away at me.

By the look on her face, I could tell she was still wavering, if not rejecting the idea altogether. I'd have to appeal to her karmic universe side. "You know what this is, right?" I asked.

"A pointless exercise that doesn't matter because Tyler insured it?" she guessed, taking another sip from the Mexican Mocha Latte I brought her with one hand while petting Lucky with the other.

I couldn't believe it wasn't super obvious. "No. This is one of those life-defining journeys. If we can find the stolen diamond before the police do, it means you're destined to marry Tyler," I said, crossing my fingers and toes while hoping I could find it.

"And if we can't find it?" she asked.

"Don't worry. We'll find it," I said with as much confidence as I could muster. It couldn't be any harder than tracking down a murderer. Could it? "Who else knew about the ring?"

"Tyler's paralegal, Melanie, who helped him rush it through customs from London. She's also the one that processed his insurance claim but other than that, no one knew," she said.

Perfect. We had one suspect. That was better than nothing. I held open the conference room door and pulled on the front of the cart while she pushed from behind. Lucky hopped up onto my shoulder for a better look around and then over to Shelby's shoulder.

We were in a massively huge, glass-walled room in the center of the library. All the tables and chairs had been moved out and replaced by a beautiful array of floor-to-ceiling, life-sized book displays, cut-out movie posters, and book excerpts. The centerpiece of the room was an enormous Harry Potter display with hand-painted glass figurines and accessories. The carefully laid-out scenes were posed for magic battles, the classroom, and the winter ball as described in the book.

"This looks amazing! You created all of this by yourself?" I asked, tracing my fingers along the colossal Quidditch field featuring suspended figurines battling it out on a makeshift playing field. She paperclipped everything carefully into the ceiling via an elaborate set-up of strings, levers, and wires.

"Yep. It took me all week," she said. "Look, I even animated it." She gently placed Lucky on the floor before flicking on the light switch in the corner.

The complex network of strings and figurines in the mock Quidditch arena suddenly came to life. The little butterfly winged ball fluttered back and forth, flying under and over different areas of the room. Unfortunately, Lucky also found it utterly fascinating. He took off at record speed, soaring through the air to catch the ball. Tangling himself in the strings on his descent, he took half the display down with him when he crashed unceremoniously into the elaborate exhibit.

"Lucky, no! Stop! Bad kitty!" I yelled, trying my best to grab him. He was in my arms for a millisecond before the winged ball zig-zagged right in front of him and shot over to another part of the room. Using me as a base, Lucky sprang into the air, tackling it while bringing the other barely standing parts of the exhibit down with him.

Completely oblivious to the destruction he left in his wake, Lucky hopped up onto the top of the table with the Quidditch ball still in his mouth. He looked from me to Shelby, waiting for kitty confirmation that he was a star before proceeding to perform some kitty somersaults, summarily knocking down the rest of the standing figurines on the table.

"Well, so much for leaving early today," said Shelby, kneeling down to pick up the decimated display pieces.

I joined her. "I am so very sorry about this," I said. Maybe I was jinxed. I was single-handedly responsible for ruining Shelby's life not once but twice in the brief span of twenty-four hours. Who comes to apologize to someone and then destroys any chance of her leaving work early in the process?

"It's fine. This is good practice for me later. Kitty owner lesson number one: never bring your cat to your makeshift quidditch room," she said, giving him a soft pat on the head when he dropped the Quidditch ball at her feet. "Good boy, Lucky. Thank you for bringing this back to me."

Basking in what Lucky perceived a good kitty deed, he proceeded to rub himself against Shelby's legs. When her phone buzzed from the other side of the room where the cart was, he dashed in front of her, causing her to trip and fall in the process.

"Kitty owner lesson number two: let the cat answer the phone first," she said when I started to apologize again as I helped her up. "I know better than to make any quick moves around Lucky."

She slowly shuffled the rest of the way over to her phone and hit the voicemail button and listened in.

I busied myself with picking up the figurines off the floor. Even though I had zero clue as to how to fix her perfectly arranged Quidditch strings, I felt committed to staying here until it was done.

After a couple minutes, she let out a little yelp as she jumped into the air.

"What is it? Did the police find your ring?" I asked. Maybe this whole diamond recovery project was for naught and the entire thing was already resolved.

"No. It's Natalia. She says she finally has an Abyssinian kitten available and it's blue, the color I've always wanted but I have to come right away to get it," she said.

"Congratulations! That's fantastic," I said, running over to give her a celebration hug. Not wanting to miss out on the fun, Lucky jumped between us and started licking our faces. "Did you hear that, Lucky? Auntie Shelby is getting a tiny, miniature, lookalike version of you so you'll have a cute, little kitty cousin to play with."

Even though he had no idea what I just said, Lucky sensed the excitement in my voice and started jumping up and down between kitty somersaults.

"Oh, wait. I can't leave yet," She dropped her shoulders in defeat and sank back onto one of the benches.

"I can stay here and fix this," I said.

"You know how to restring a mock animated Quidditch field?" she asked, already knowing the answer.

"Well, maybe I can pick the kitten up for you," I said, scooping Lucky back up and luring him into his carrier with some kitty treats.

"Really? Are you sure?" asked Shelby, biting her lower lip.

"It's the very least I can do," I said. Like, the very least.

"All right, but you'll have to hurry. Natalia said there was another person interested so the cat goes to whoever shows up first," she said.

I wondered how firm that forty miles per hour speed limit was? What was the worst that could happen if I pushed it just a little beyond that amount?

7

After securing Lucky's kitty carrier in the backseat, I locked the back door and hopped into the driver's seat to make a silent plea to the car.

"I promise to take you to the repair shop if you'll just make this one trip for me," I said to the car before hitting the start button. It revved to life as if it understood. With a silent vow to the universe to never miss another oil change appointment again, I promised to uphold my end of the bargain if the car would just make it there and back at sixty miles per hour.

All went well until about ten minutes outside of Bangor when the car started making some weird, sputtering sounds. I was so close. This couldn't be happening! I eased off the accelerator, dropping the speed to the recommended forty and the sounds (thankfully) went away. I exhaled a huge sigh of relief.

At that speed, it took another thirty minutes to get to Bangor. I called Natalia to make sure the other competing kitty buyers hadn't arrived yet and she advised me to hurry. I held my breath as I drove the car at thirty-nine miles per hour exactly. A big plus of going so slow is: there was no traffic. It felt like forever but I finally made it. Natalia's place was just as I remembered it. Chock full of cute, adorable Abyssinian kittens that Natalia bred and lovable Labrador puppies that her sister bred.

"You know that one cat is good luck but two means you will die a lonely spinster," said Natalia in her thick Russian accent.

"Well, thank you for that sage dating advice but the second kitten is for my friend, Shelby, remember?" I replied, putting Lucky down on the ground so he could play with all the new kittens and puppies that were not here the last time we came.

"Sure, a friend," said Natalia, patting me on the shoulder. "Maybe you would like a puppy instead?" She reached down and grabbed one of the chocolate Labs, which she placed in my hands. The puppy was super excited and started licking not only my face, but my neck, my hair, and my ear. He let out cute, little puppy yelps.

"Thanks but I can barely take care of Lucky," I said, placing the pup down gently on the couch.

Natalia handed me another puppy, this time, a black one. "Maybe you like this color better?" The black puppy barked and exhibited a much more lively personality. He crawled up onto my shoulder and bravely jumped onto the couch himself, joining the other Lab for a wrestling session.

"Or maybe you prefer the traditional yellow color?" she asked, putting yet another puppy in my arms. This one seemed scared and shell-shocked, obviously unfamiliar with being held by anyone so I quickly placed him back on the ground where Lucky ambushed him before playing with him. He recoiled, clearly not enjoying this new encounter. He was definitely not the puppy for me and Lucky.

"They're all very cute but I think I'll just stick with the kitten that you said you had."

"Which one do you want? I expect a new litter next month or do you still want the blue one that was returned?" she asked.

She pointed to the silver and grey Abyssinian in the corner, hiding under the blanket. "Why was he returned?" I asked. Shelby never mentioned anything about a returned kitten.

"He's a she and yes, she was returned because she's a runt, and never grew beyond that size," she said.

"But she's the same size as Lucky," I said, comparing the two.

"Oh, right. You can return him, too, but I don't give refunds. Do you want to return?" she asked.

"No. I just meant, he seems average size to me," I said. But now that I thought about it, Lucky did still fit into his baby kitty bjorn that I bought him when he was a tiny kitten four months ago. I guessed this was what happened when you grew up without any pets and had absolutely no knowledge about them. I assumed he would eventually reach full size in a couple of years or so. I took Lucky to the vet for his shots when I first got him but hadn't returned since then. They said he was the normal size and weight for his age at the time.

"If you like his size then he is normal size for you. There's always a runt in every litter but I guess this time, there are two," she said, shrugging it off. "It sounds like she is the perfect size cat for you. They would be a good matching pair, no?"

I was about to repeat that the kitten was for Shelby but Natalia had already decided I was tragically destined for lonely spinsterhood, surrounded by cats. It was possible she was right.

I kneeled down and slowly made my way to the small, blue kitten under the blanket. She peeked one eye out but stayed exactly where she was. I extended my hand out, palm up, towards her left paw.

"Hey there, little girl. I promise I'm friendly. Are you scared?" I asked, sliding my hand under her paw. She didn't move away, which was a good sign.

Lucky hopped over to inspect what was going on and sniffed the paw in my hand. Not wanting to waste any time to slowly introduce himself, he crawled under the covers to join her, even snuggling up with her. It was actually super cute. Now, I felt bad at having to separate them. Maybe Natalia was right. I was destined for a lonely spinster future teeming with cats, which, now that I thought about it, didn't sound so bad. They were cute, they were cuddly, and they were super loving. I wondered why being a cat owner got such a bad rap. And why just women? No one ever plastered derogatory dating status labels on single men with cats.

"What's her name?" I asked.

"Defective," said Natalia. It was a good thing these kittens were so cute on their own. Natalia's retail skills left more than a little to be desired.

"Didn't the previous owners that returned her give her a name?" I asked. Even if you chose to return a kitten, you usually would have called it something besides *Kitty*.

"Four-oh-seven," said Natalia.

"They gave her four hundred and seven different names?" I asked. I'd heard of indecisive people but that was beyond ridiculous.

"No. That was her name. Cat number four-oh-seven. They bought her to show in competitions. That's why they had to return her. She's defective," said Natalia.

"Oh, you're not defective, little girl. We'll call you Skye, because you're blue," I said.

Lucky flicked some of the covers off and started licking the blue kitten, who immediately licked him back. It looked like they were bosom buddies. "I'll take her," I said.

"Shelby still owes me four thousand dollars," said Natalia.

"Didn't she give you a deposit?" I asked. Shelby mentioned there was a balance. I tried calling and texting her but she wasn't picking up. I didn't know what to do. If I didn't pay the money, Natalia would offer Skye to the next person but if I overpaid, it would be unfair to ask Shelby to cover my mistake. I already ruined her engagement proposal and her library display. If I failed to get her Skye, I'd officially go down as the worst friend in history.

"Did she? I don't remember," said Natalia, looking up at the ceiling vacantly.

Four thousand seemed like a lot for a returned kitten that Natalia kept referring to as defective. I was so worried about the car's capped speed limit, I forgot to ask Shelby how much she'd already paid before taking off.

"Can we wait until Shelby calls me back?" I asked, pacing the room. I tried calling Shelby again but was interrupted by a knock on the door.

Oh, no! The other buyers. I grabbed Natalia's arm to stop her from answering the door and asked, "Do you take Venmo?"

Venmo had a three thousand dollar limit so I had to shave a thousand off the price. Natalia seemed surprised when I didn't try to haggle so she probably wasn't expecting to even get that much for the blue kitten. Not to mention her *no refund* policy, which meant she'd already been paid four thousand dollars for Skye in the original sale.

The person at the door was simply the mailman delivering a package. It figured.

I carefully placed Lucky and Skye together in Lucky's kitty carrier. Having purchased the larger size, I expected Lucky would grow into it but seeing how he never did (or would), it was perfect for both cats to lie in comfortably.

When I turned to thank Natalia before leaving, she placed another puppy in my arms. This was a silver Labrador. "I see you like the blue color. Maybe you want this one?" she asked. "He could be Skye number two?"

"I didn't know Labradors came in blue," I said as the puppy got excited and licked my face.

"They don't. That's a Weimaraner. We're trying to expand our brand," she said. "You want? I give you a special price."

The next time Shelby decided to get a kitten, maybe I should suggest she send a courier to retrieve it. This puppy was so adorable, I could feel my heart melting with each puppy breath lick on my face. "Aww, he's really cute but I probably shouldn't." I wanted to put him down but his eyes were such a bright blue. They pierced my puppy soul, telling me to bring him home.

"Sure you do not have another friend who needs a special, loving pet?" she asked, emphasizing the word *friend*. "It gets lonely on weekends when you are single, no?"

"But my daily Venmo amount is maxed out today," I said, snuggling against the Weimaraner's face.

"Okay. Well, you know where to find me when your Venmo account works again," she replied, snatching the puppy out of my arms.

I gasped. Not that the Labs weren't super cute but that Weimaraner was sheer out-of-control puppy power in its caliber of cuteness. Good thing I came here alone. If Shelby were with me, she'd say it was a sign I was destined to get a puppy today and even spot me the money to buy him.

8

I popped open the hatchback on my parents' Hyundai Santa Fe. The car was perfect now, if you ignored the whole oil change mishap. I outfitted the back with a doggy gate and net so that Lucky could stay safely contained in the back while I was driving and get plenty of airflow. I retrofitted the walls with extra padding in case of an accident so it was a good compromise between kitty safety and kitty comfort.

"All right, car. You just have to make it back home to Clover Creek and first thing tomorrow, I will take you in for an oil change," I said, bargaining with the car as if it could understand or even cared.

"Guess who's in my car and dying to meet her new kitty mommy?" I asked the car speakerphone on my drive back from Bangor. I intended to drive straight to Shelby's apartment on the wharf and drop Skye off with her. She lived in a fancy high-rise next door to the Highland Yacht Club. "We're on our way to your place now."

"I'm not there. I'm actually at the pet store over on

Lowell Avenue stocking up on kitty supplies but I'm almost done," she said.

"You already have an entire bedroom dedicated to the cat. What more could you possibly need?" I asked. Shopping for cat trees, cat beds, cat toys, and catnip had become a new hobby for Shelby. It was a good thing she lived alone in a two-bedroom apartment or else she'd never have enough room to hold all of the cat stuff she kept buying while waiting for a Lucky lookalike Abyssinian to become available.

"Oh, you know, just some necessities like kitty tee shirts and kitty booties," she said.

"But it's summertime," I reminded her. Not to mention that cats weren't exactly into getting dressed up. Lucky loved dressing up. He had his own closet filled with kitty pajamas, kitty sweaters, kitty socks, and even kitty costumes for Halloween but Lucky was weird. I wasn't sure Skye would share the same fondness for being dressed up like a Barbie doll as Lucky did. And even then, he only did it during the winter when it was cold. We were now well into June and increasingly warmer weather.

"Winter will be here before you know it and since it's summer, all the winter pet clothing is on sale," she explained. Sound logic I couldn't argue with.

"Hey, do you want to meet me at my place when you're done since it's right down the street from the pet store?" I asked.

"As long as you promise we can order in a deep dish from Malnati's with the works. I'm starving from all this kitty clearance clothes shopping," she said.

That was music to my ears. "Done," I said. "Do you have a kitty carrier for the car?"

I heard some shuffling on the other end. "I do now," she said.

The car made a loud bang and proceeded to shut itself off.

"What was that?" asked Shelby.

"Nothing," I said, easing the car onto the shoulder of the road. "It's the radio. Hey, let me call you back."

Luckily, I was far enough out of Bangor that I wasn't stranded in the middle of a busy intersection, blocking traffic like earlier this morning. And instead of taking the highway, I'd opted for the backroads into town where I could drive at a lower speed. There was nothing but grass for miles. It looked like I was out in farm country, specifically, goat country.

I made a few more attempts to plead with the car to start but it ignored me. Forty-five miles was too far to walk the rest of the way. My only choice was to call for help.

If I called AAA again, my dad would know I didn't change the oil on time like I was supposed to. If I called Ruby, she'd know I didn't listen to her advice to take the car in and besides, she didn't have keys to her car to come get me anyway. I already ruined most of Shelby's weekend so I hated to admit to her that I was stranded with her new kitten on the side of the road in the middle of nowhere. That left Marcus. I dialed his number and crossed my fingers that he was at the Bangor airport and headed back to Clover Creek.

"Hi, Ava, I just landed. Can I call you back when I get to Clover Creek?" asked Marcus.

Hooray! At least one thing was going my way.

"Actually, that's what I was calling you for. I'm having a little car trouble. Any chance I can get a lift back home with you?" I asked. "I'm near you, about fifteen minutes south of the airport."

"Of course. I can see your coordinates now," he said. "I'll be there in five minutes."

There were perks to having a tech billionaire genius as your friend. He gave you his company's Palmer Tech Smartwatch, which had GPS on it. He may not have been my boyfriend but he was still a pretty great friend.

I texted Shelby to let her know I was running a little late and would call her when I had a better estimate of my arrival time.

When I came around the back, Lucky and Skye didn't even seem to notice we stopped. Lucky was usually dying to get out and scratching away at the window. But instead, they were both wrestling around and tumbling over each other when I opened the hatch. I easily tucked them both into the kitty carrier together again. They seemed happy to be anywhere as long as they were with each other.

I slung the kitty carrier over my shoulder and had just closed the back when a huge gust of wind practically blew me away.

The source of the hurricane was a fancy looking helicopter in Palmer Tech brand colors of royal blue and gold. The door opened and Marcus stepped out, looking just as handsome as the last time I saw him. His dark ebony skin was flawless and his chiseled features made him perfect for a fashion magazine photoshoot. Despite the fancy mode of transportation, he had on khaki shorts, a heather grey tee shirt, and flip-flops.

"Do you always use a helicopter to get to and from the airport?" I screamed as loud as I could to be heard over the helicopter propellers.

"Yes, it's much faster," said Marcus with his classic, boy-next-door smile, as if traveling by helicopter were simply a matter of trying to be more productive. "Is someone coming to take care of the car?"

Oh, right. The car. I could deal with that later. Possibly tomorrow. I waved it off and simply nodded my head yes.

"Great, are you ready to go?" he asked,

As ready as I ever could be to travel in a helicopter. On the plus side, I didn't have to worry about being late in getting back home.

Marcus put a pair of big earmuff headphones on me so we could talk. I balanced the kitty carrier on my lap. The helicopter noise, combined with the new smells and sights, stopped the cats from what they were doing. They were now wide-eyed and curious to see where we were. It was too loud to say anything comforting so I just looked at them and smiled. They seemed confused but content to be with each other.

I brought Marcus up to speed on the missing diamond ring, my forgotten oil change, and the new kitten retrieval.

"Nice! A diamond heist," said Marcus, giving me a high five.

I returned his high five but wondered how that was good news. "But it was heisted on my watch," I said.

"Exactly. All the good things happen to you," said Marcus, giving me a wink.

"I'm not sure I'd file this under the good category of life events," I said. Was this Marcus's idea of a pep talk?

"What are you talking about? This is perfect. You know how we love solving puzzles and mysteries together. I'm going to call my assistant now and have her clear my schedule for the week so we can figure this out together," he said, already tapping away at his Smartwatch.

The helicopter engine cut off. How were we already back in Clover Creek and at Marcus's house? When he saw the shocked look on my face, he explained that his helicopter was a special military grade design that went faster than normal speeds.

I handed the kitty carrier to Marcus and followed him out

of the helicopter on what felt like the middle of the ocean. In addition to being a super cool, secret, underwater ocean lair, it looked like Marcus's house also had a special helipad that sprang up from the ocean floor. Now I knew what billionaires did with all their money. They bought ridiculously impressive toys that made their lives ultraconvenient. He asked me when we first met if he could give me a ride home in his helicopter. Until now, I kind of assumed he was joking.

"I feel like I'm in a spy movie," I said to Marcus as I followed him down the helipad into a secret door in the ground.

"That's precisely what I was going for. I always loved James Bond as a kid. It's kind of why I started designing gadgets in the first place," he said. That made sense. I vaguely recalled him mentioning that before but I was so mesmerized by his ultra white teeth and Hollywood good looks that I probably wasn't even listening. "Double-oh-seven had one of these and I've always wanted one of my own."

The secret oval opening from the helipad flowed into a long, winding staircase. But not the creepy, haunted house kind. This one was completely encased in triply reinforced glass (or at least, I hoped it was triply reinforced in case a great white shark smashed into it), just like his house, and surrounded by all sorts of glow-in-the-dark plants. Deep blue mushroom-shaped plants beside purple and pink, huge, sunflower-shaped plants, and violet plants with glowing white centers along with other strange shapes and colors were interspersed all the way to the house entrance door.

"Wow, all of these plants are so beautiful," I said, taking my time and keeping up with him. I didn't even know anything grew under saltwater besides kelp. It looked like a huge box of glow-in-the-dark crayons. I was almost sad when we reached his house.

I followed him into what looked like his closet. Seeing the odd expression on my face, he answered before I had a chance to ask. "Yes, this is my closet. I would've shown you the plants the last time you were here but since we just met each other, I feared it might have seemed a little creepy if I asked to show you something in the back of my closet."

"Good call," I said. The walkway view was nothing short of amazing but I was already thoroughly impressed with his actual house. Being invited into his bedroom, and then shoved into a dark closet might make me think he was casting me out as dinner for his pet shark or something.

I'd been here before but was just as impressed this time around as I was the first time. It made me feel like I was inside the world's fanciest aquarium, which I kind of was.

"Let me grab something from my office and I'll drive you home," said Marcus, heading to his office downstairs.

Marcus came down the stairs with a dozen red roses and held them out to me.

"Here, these are for you," he said. "They're a little late but I hope you can still enjoy them."

A million little butterflies traveled up my spine, making me all tingly.

"Thanks, but late for what?" I asked, taking the flowers and inhaling their perfume scent.

"I felt bad when you mistook Lila's bouquet of plastic flowers as being intended for you and honestly, I should have gotten you some before now so these are late flowers," he said.

The butterflies dissipated, replaced by burning embarrassment. The last time Marcus and I were together in his car, I mistook the beauty pageant prop he brought for his sister, Lila, as a romantic gesture to me from him. Not only was it mortifying then, it was doubly worse now.

"Oh, I see," I said, simply nodding and staring at the flowers while avoiding eye contact. These were Band-Aid flowers to heal my wounded ego, not romantic flowers.

9

Fifteen minutes later, I was outside my front door. Shelby was en route and expected any minute.

"Do you want to get started on that diamond theft investigation tonight?" asked Marcus. I could tell he wanted to come inside and meet Skye outside of the kitty carrier and hang out. But I couldn't stop thinking how silly I felt with the whole rose bouquet he was compelled to purchase for me due to our prior misunderstanding.

"Thanks for the rescue ride home but I'm actually really tired. Rain check?" I asked.

He looked a little disappointed at my response but recovered quickly. "Sure, of course. I have lots of unpacking and laundry to do," he said, even though we both knew he had people who did his laundry for him.

"Well, have fun," I said, hopping out of the car and shutting the door before he had a chance to reply. It was kind of rude, considering he rescued me from a stranded car outside Bangor but I felt like a charity case after the way he gave me the roses instead of a romantic interest.

"Come on, Lucky. Let's show Skye your house and all of your kitty toys inside," I said, dropping the flowers in the foyer and focusing all my attention on the kitty carrier as I heard Marcus pulling away behind me.

I gently guided Lucky and Skye to the main room to play and explore. If you didn't know it, you'd think my house was a cat sanctuary judging by all the kitty tunnels I installed that ran along the walls. There were at least two cat trees in every room and a kitty tunnel sitting on every rug. Each of the windows was outfitted with kitty perches and random kitty toys cluttered the whole place. Lucky had a toy box and knew how to put his toys away when he was done with them but I was pretty lax when it came to enforcing rules and discipline.

Skye vacillated between being happy and excited about all the kitty toys to looking scared and trying to hide under the blanket on the couch. I couldn't blame her. It was pretty overwhelming, especially considering she was rejected by her first set of kitty parents. What kind of heartless person could abandon something so fluffy and sweet?

Lucky did a good job as an older brother in showing Skye around so I went into the kitchen to make Shelby and me some drinks. I just finished pouring us a couple of root beer floats when the doorbell rang. Putting them into the freezer, I went to answer the door. As expected, Lucky beat me there and was jumping up and down excitedly when he saw Shelby through the frosted glass pane. Skye wasn't nearly as adventurous and stayed safely behind the couch, watching and observing her from afar, only briefly showing her cute, little blue face as she peeked out over the tops of the cushions.

"Are you ready to meet the new love of your life?" I asked, hoping it wasn't too over the top. That was pretty much how I felt about Lucky and I wasn't even a cat person.

Lucky immediately crawled up her legs and got into her arms, giving her a Lucky-style hello, full of kitty face licks and cuddles even though he'd just seen her a few hours ago. "How is my favorite little kitty doing?" she cooed into his ear while scratching his neck. Lucky found kitty heaven with Shelby. "Or I guess I should say, how is one of my favorite little kitties doing now that there are two Luckys?"

"Are you ready to meet your new kitty mommy?" I asked Skye, gently pulling back the covers to reveal her tiny, little, blue kitten face. Skye seemed surprised at being so swiftly exposed but Lucky immediately jumped over and shielded her with his tiny kitty body. He was like the perfect older brother you always wanted on your side.

"Ohmigosh, she's so cute. I love her already," said Shelby, kneeling down on the floor until she was eye level with Skye. Skye peeked one eye out curiously at Shelby but stayed hidden behind Lucky. To show her that Shelby was safe, Lucky went over and licked Shelby's hand before rubbing himself against her arm. "She looks just like Lucky but blue."

"I've been calling her Skye since she didn't have a name but you can change it to whatever you want," I said, still mortified at the thought of calling a cat a number.

"I love the name, Skye, it's perfect," she replied, tears rolling down her face. "Thank you so much for going to pick her up."

She leaned over and gave me a hug, which was totally undeserved, considering I allowed Lucky to destroy her entire Harry Potter exhibit, as the reason she couldn't pick Skye up herself. Not wanting to miss out, Lucky jumped between us. Refusing to be ignored, Skye pawed Shelby's side. She didn't jump in like Lucky but she was definitely curious about what we were doing.

"Hi there, Skye. I'm your new mommy and I'm going to make sure you live your best kitty life ever," said Shelby, repositioning herself so she was eye level with Skye. She softly rubbed the kitten's face and then looked up at me. "I got your voicemails and Venmo'd you the three thousand."

"Is that what you agreed upon with Natalia? I'm so sorry if I overpaid her but I did shave a thousand off her original asking price," I said.

Shelby waved her hand in the air, dismissing it. "It was a little more than she quoted me but seeing this adorable little face is worth all the money in the world."

That was exactly how I felt about Lucky. He was my little guy! Staying in on a Friday night, watching the Hallmark Channel, snugly cuddled up together on the couch was better than anything I could buy. I wouldn't trade this little guy for all the money in the world. I picked him up and cradled him against my chest for a little kitty hug.

"Are you thinking what I'm thinking?" I asked Shelby.

"If you're thinking we should order our deep dish pizza stat, then yes," she replied.

That was actually a fantastic idea. I was a little disappointed I hadn't thought to order it as soon as I walked in the door. "Wonderful idea! Let's put our order into Malnati's now and while we wait, we can put together a whiteboard of diamond theft suspects," I said.

"I'm with you on the pizza ordering but why would we want to whiteboard suspects?" asked Shelby.

"Why not? It could be fun," I retorted. I was probably the only person who classified putting together a suspect list as a fun way to spend a Saturday night. Except for Marcus, who now saw me as a pathetic, lonely spinster in need of pity roses.

"I don't know if I'd call that fun but as long as we can eat Malnati's deep dish while doing so, sure. I'll help. What do you need from me?" asked Shelby, tossing a piece of string between Skye and Lucky.

"Great! You order the pizza and I'll get the whiteboard set up," I answered. I headed to the kitchen and gathered the whiteboard and dry erase markers from the kitchen and propped them up in the living room.

"Should we add breadsticks and garlic butter dipping sauce?" she inquired, entering the order on her phone.

"Like you need to ask," I said. Life was too short to pass up any carbs.

I wrote SUSPECTS in all caps across the top in blue and added Melanie, Kira and Doug underneath. "Kira was there when Tyler dropped it off. Dale the Dairy Farmer delivered some milk that day and left it in the fridge but there's no way he knew there was a diamond stashed in the safe," I said.

"We can obviously cross Kira off the list. She's the nicest person ever. I can't imagine her stealing anything," said Shelby. Jealousy was definitely something only I suffered from. Shelby had no issue with Tyler and Kira remaining friends, despite their past dating status. The urge to tell her what Kira said about boyfriends being up for grabs was nearly killing me but that wouldn't solve anything. Plus, Kira seemed way more interested in stealing Wesley away from his girlfriend than recycling her ex.

"So our only suspects are Melanie and Dale?" I asked, taking a step back from the whiteboard.

"Did you forget about Lucky? He was there and knew all about the diamond ring, didn't you, little guy?" replied Shelby, clearly way more interested in kitty playtime than crime-busting clues. Although I'd probably be the same way if it were my first night with a new kitten.

"Kira said she didn't see anything unusual that day but maybe Dale did when he dropped off the milk," I said, making a note to ask him about any witnesses. "It was locked up in the safe all day but maybe someone broke in." Or worse. Maybe I forgot to lock it? That seemed unlikely but I never used the safe before. What if I closed it wrong and left it open?

"Who else has the combination?" asked Shelby, using the blanket to play peek-a-boo with Skye and Lucky.

"Just Ruby, who obviously would never steal it," I said, not even bothering to put her name on the whiteboard. "But Chloe did install it for me and Grant purchased it originally for his sister, who owned the bakery before me. Grant is in prison but maybe Chloe knows something about the safe that I don't. Like, maybe there's a master key or some master lock hacker visiting Clover Creek," I said.

"That's a good start, right?" asked Shelby, looking at our whiteboard.

"Yes, thanks for your help," I said, capping the dry erase marker. "I almost forgot the best part." I ran back to the kitchen to retrieve our root beer floats from the freezer.

Handing one of the frosty mugs to Shelby, I took a seat on the couch opposite her with the kittens wrestling on the blanket between us.

"Nice. Root beer floats are my favorite," said Shelby, spooning a huge mound of root beer-covered vanilla ice cream into her mouth and moaning her appreciation.

"Congratulations on becoming a new kitty mommy," I said, raising my mug to hers for a toast. I slurped down a big gulp from the straw before switching over to the spoon inside the glass.

"You know who's missing from the board?" asked Shelby.

I jumped up and uncapped the dry erase marker, ready to add to the list.

"Madame Omega, my psychic. She predicted all of this would happen a week ago," said Shelby.

10

After our kitty and pizza sleepover, Shelby and I decided to divide and conquer the next day. Shelby would check if Tyler's paralegal, Melanie, might have told anyone about the diamond ring and I'd find out if Dale the Dairy Farmer saw anything out of the ordinary. We planned to reconvene back at my place at six PM.

Lucky and Skye were not happy about splitting up for the day. Lucky was pretty much a silent cat but when he saw Shelby heading out the door with Skye in her arms, he let out a sad, little kitty mewl and ran out the door after her.

"Don't worry, little guy. We'll see Skye all the time," I said, picking him up and cradling him in my arms like a baby.

"That's odd. I don't remember seeing your car parked out here when I arrived last night. Did you move it from the garage to the outside this morning?" asked Shelby, pointing to my parents' SUV, which I abandoned yesterday on the side of the road outside Bangor.

"That's because it wasn't here last night," I said, running up to the car.

"Look, there's an envelope on it. Is it a parking ticket?" asked Shelby, following me to the dashboard and peering over my shoulder as I opened it.

Ava was written in a big, black Sharpie marker on the front. The envelope had the monogram *MP* on the flap. There was a matching cream-colored card inside with a note from Marcus: *Flew back to retrieve your car for you. I replaced the broken head gaskets and gave it a full tune-up. It should be working like new now. Marcus.*

"Nice. Your boyfriend beats mine. Tyler has never once taken my car in for a repair, oil change or tune-up," said Shelby, gently placing Skye in her car before she slid into the driver's seat.

"He's not my boyfriend," I said, tucking the card back into its envelope. "We're just friends."

"Are you sure about that?" asked Shelby. "I saw those roses in the foyer you didn't bother to mention."

"Those were just pity flowers because he felt sorry for me," I said.

She gave me a weird look but didn't press further when I made it obvious I was done with that topic.

Boyfriends gave women flowers just because, or for a special occasion, or to say thank you; not to console their bruised ego. I waved goodbye to Shelby as she pulled away.

Lucky stared intently at Shelby's car and whimpered when she drove away. "Don't worry, we have plenty of stuff to keep us busy today. You won't even notice she's gone."

It was Sunday so Frosted was closed but I had plenty of cupcake ingredients in my kitchen at home. I threw on an apron and baked Dale's favorite cupcakes, my Pumpkin Spiced Caramel Cupcakes with Cream Cheese Filling and headed out to his dairy farm with Lucky.

I didn't think he stole the ring but he might've seen or heard something that could be helpful. He was always very quiet when he delivered the milk. He parked in the back, wheeled it into the fridge, and took off before I ever knew he was there. I had no complaints, though. We'd never once ran out of milk since I stopped hauling milk cartons from the grocery store and opened an account with Dale. Billing was done completely online and the orders were pretty steady for the last month; so unless I was in the back when he delivered the milk, we never actually talked very much.

There were no milk deliveries on weekends so I'd have to go to Dale if I wanted answers before his next delivery on Monday. The dairy farm was situated at the outer edge of town on a large, twenty-acre plot right near the county fairgrounds, which was a good twenty-minute drive.

I'd never been here before and neither had Lucky but he immediately acted like he was right at home. As soon as I opened the car door, he bounced out of his kitty bjorn before I could stop him and ran over to join the cows in the field. I set the cupcakes I brought on top of the car hood and chased after him at significantly less than warp speed. I feared he could get trampled by the cows. He was so tiny and they were so big.

"Lucky, stop! Lucky, heel! Lucky, come back!" I yelled, trying every command I could think of, all of which he ignored. I really needed to take him back to doggy obedience classes. I came up to one of those old-style, wooden log fences, intended to keep cows confined but certainly not kittens. On the plus side, the fence was pretty easy to scale for me at five-foot-eleven. On the minus side, the smell in there was nothing like a cupcake bakery.

By the time I caught up to Lucky, he had latched onto a cow that seemed smitten with him. They took turns grooming each other. The cow lay down on the ground and they actually cuddled together. I never visited a dairy farm. I was out sick the day the school took a field trip to a dairy so this was really my first time being around cows. Who knew they were so gentle and affectionate? The other cows didn't really seem to mind that I was there either.

I had to head up to the main house to find Dale. Lucky was okay and looked pretty happy to be hanging out with the cows but I was still leery about leaving him out there unsupervised with animals that weighed a gazillion times more than he did.

"C'mon, little guy. You can come back and visit your new friend after we find Dale," I said, scooping him up and placing him into his little kitty bjorn. When I picked him up, a thousand super long, bright green grass blades came with him. I tried to collect them but they were everywhere, not just on Lucky but all over my shoes and pant bottoms. I was glad I was dressed super casually today. Lucky looked listless and tried to extricate himself so I had to give up my grass collection in order to secure him in place with both hands.

It took me longer to get out of the cow pasture than it did to enter it. I looked for the gate this time, which was higher up on the hill, and a good five hundred feet away. Even though Lucky was only four pounds, he felt like forty at my current uphill hiking fitness level, not to mention the tall grass I had to stomp and weave through. I saw Dale at the edge of the fencepost and hollered up at him.

"Hey, Dale, it's Ava," I called, waving one of my arms while holding Lucky in place with the other. I didn't want him to think I was a trespasser and shoot me.

Sitting on a rocking chair with his hat covering his face, I assumed he must've fallen asleep. I couldn't blame him. Watching cows graze was only so exciting. Struggling to suck in enough air, I was wheezing by the time I reached him so my *hey, Dale* probably sounded more like a *heykul*. I opened the gate and gently shook him awake.

"I brought your favorite cupcakes," I said. Technically, the Pumpkin Spiced Caramel Cupcakes with Cream Cheese Filling were a good distance away, at the edge of the dairy farm on top of the car. Maybe Dale would walk me out to retrieve them so I wouldn't have to hike back up this hill again.

When he didn't respond, I lifted his hat to wake him up and saw lifeless eyes staring back at me. I screamed and dropped the hat immediately.

"Dale?" I said, already aware he wouldn't respond. Not now or ever again. I checked his pulse all the same, just to be sure but there was nothing. He was ice cold and not because of the brisk morning air.

Did he have a heart attack? Could he have died of old age at the ripe, young year of forty-nine? I was about to call out for someone but remembered it was Sunday. Dale mentioned that he only had help at the farm during the week when he went out to make his deliveries. I walked behind the rocking chair and saw a huge arrow sticking out of his back, like he'd been murdered by Robin Hood.

Poor Dale. He never saw it coming. Some coward had the audacity to shoot him in the back while he was sitting on his rocker, looking after his cows. Who goes around with a bow and arrow killing dairy farmers? Especially in the twenty-first century!

Lucky was licking my face. I looked down and realized he was licking the tears that were suddenly falling down my cheeks. I barely even knew Dale. Only quite recently, I managed to get enough business to warrant large orders directly from a dairy farm. Dale was a good twenty years older than me so we didn't really run in the same social circles, either. He inherited the farm from his parents and never married or had any kids, at least, none that I knew of. So it was just him and the cows out here on the farm.

I ran, or rather, lightly jogged down to my car to get my cell phone and call the police. In my haste to chase after Lucky, I left everything down there. The downhill jog was much easier than the uphill one. But it looked like I wouldn't have to call anyone. Wesley was already pulling into the dairy farm, next to my car, as I came down the road.

By the time I reached him, I was once again out of breath. Wesley and another man I didn't recognize got out of the car. I pointed up to the top of the hill and said, "Dead. Dale's dead. Someone killed him."

"Seriously, Decker? Again?" asked Wesley, already taking off at Olympic sprinter speed up the hill.

"Don't worry. I will definitely start locking my doors again." I yelled after him, hunched over with both hands on my knees, still trying to catch my breath.

11

Oh, no. Where would I get my milk from now on? And was I a terrible person for worrying about that at a time like this? And who would take care of the cows now? I could not take in any more strays. Lucky was already a full-time job.

According to Wesley, Dale spotted someone suspicious in the alley outside Frosted when he came by with his dairy delivery on Friday. Wesley came here so Dale could identify the person he saw to a sketch artist. Whoever that person was had to be the diamond thief. Now, the perp killed the only living witness who could possibly identify them. On the plus side, this meant Shelby and I were right in our decision to ask Dale what he saw, if anything.

Clover Creek was a small town with little to no crime so the police force didn't keep a sketch artist on staff. That's what the sketch artist told me while we waited at the bottom of the hill for Wesley to check on Dale. He was the only sketch artist for all of Blueberry Bay and was busy with another murder yesterday. Otherwise, he said he would've come out sooner since time was a crucial factor in these situations.

While I was talking to the sketch artist, Lucky managed to escape from his kitty bjorn and mosey back over to his friend in the cow pasture. I excused myself to go check on him. Lucky loved going to the dog park so he probably assumed the cows were really big dogs. I found them exactly as I did before. They both resumed their prior cow and kitty cuddles like nothing happened.

"Are you okay?" asked Wesley once he finished surveying the scene and taking photos. He started picking the grass from my clothes and face. "Did you fall down in the cow pasture?"

"It's because of Lucky. He made a new friend," I said, pointing down to him and his new cuddle buddy. Before this, I had no idea cows could be so cute.

"You'll need a hose to get it all off yourself. Cow pasture grass isn't like regular grass. It's very sticky," he said, flicking some more strands off my shoulder.

"I was planning to do it anyway. I'm not really into the whole dairy farm aroma," I said, wiping away the last of my tears and a few more strands of cow grass. I concentrated on inhaling deep, steady breaths.

"Hey, what were you doing at Dale's dairy farm on a Sunday morning? Are you two close?" asked Wesley, raising his eyebrows to imply that maybe we were dating.

"Ew, gross. He's old enough to be my dad," I replied. Dale was a super nice guy but I never thought of him that way. I relegated him to that older, *dad* generation of men that watched football together and screamed at the TV while snacking on the seven-layer dip my mother made for them.

"Please do not tell me you came here to investigate on

your own after I explicitly told you to stay out of it," said Wesley, pinching the bridge of his nose and closing his eyes.

"Of course, not. I had some extra cupcakes from yesterday and I knew they were Dale's favorite so I thought I'd drop them off just to be nice," I said. It sounded totally plausible, except that I'd never done that before ever for any other vendor.

"Uh-huh," said Wesley, completely unconvinced. "This may have started out as an ordinary jewelry heist that you wanted to go poking around in but now it's turned into a homicide investigation."

"So you believe the two crimes are connected?" I asked. I thought that, too. I knew very little about Dale, besides what a shy, quiet guy he was but I found it hard to believe someone would hate him enough to kill him unless he might have witnessed something important.

"Most likely. Look, stop trying to figure this out. If you had been here when the killer was, you could've been lying dead right next to him," said Wesley, like that could scare me. I overcame a man holding me at gunpoint, outwitted a crazy beauty pageant queen while suspended thirty feet in the air and survived a car crash in a potato field. Nothing scared me anymore. Except accidentally buying another kitten or puppy from Natalia.

Before he could berate me further, the same crime scene unit that was in Frosted on Friday night arrived on the scene. I offered them what were supposed to be Dale's dozen cupcakes, which they accepted with a smile. I couldn't bear to take them back home.

"In case you're wondering, I have an alibi for the time of the murder," I said, walking back over to Wesley. I overheard the coroner announce *last night at five PM* as the time of Dale's death.

"Of course, you do. Go ahead," he said, opening up his notepad and clicking his ballpoint pen.

"Like usual, Ruby woke me up super early at nine and we headed over to her parents' house for Pancake Towers but my car died right outside of Town Square on Main Street so I had to call AAA, which took so long that Ruby's father had to toss them---" I rattled off before Wesley interrupted me.

"Decker, I just need your five PM alibi, not a minute-by-minute description of your entire day," said Wesley, crinkling his forehead and pinching his nose again.

"At five PM, I was in a helicopter with a friend," I said.

"Are you referring to your boyfriend, Marcus Palmer?" asked Wesley.

"He's not my boyfriend. My car died and he just happened to be flying by so he gave me a ride," I said. Saying it out loud sounded even sillier than it did in my head. Why couldn't Dale have been killed earlier in the day when my alibi did not have to include Marcus?

"Uh-huh. I bet he gives all of his friends rides in his private helicopter," said Marcus, writing it down on his notepad.

Wesley seemed ready to usher me out of here, which was just fine by me. I was more than eager for a fresh shower. I gently disentangled Lucky from the cow's embrace and plopped him back into his kitty bjorn. He tried to escape again but I held him in place. I made a mental note to buy him a cow stuffed animal for home. That seemed much safer.

Wesley followed me out of the cow pasture and down the hill to my car, or rather, my parents' car. Lucky whimpered the whole time, standing up in my arms and looking at his cow friend over my shoulder. The cow followed us right to the edge of the fence. I let them say goodbye with a few more cow-kitty licks before pulling Lucky away. He let out a sad, little kitty mewl.

I popped open the hatchback on my parents' Hyundai Santa Fe and gently placed Lucky inside, pulling up the baby gate so it enclosed the hatchback opening. He rubbed his wet kitty nose against the glass, making sad streak marks as he looked longingly at his cow friend, staring back at him from the pasture. He let out some despondent kitty mewls at not being able to participate in more cow-kitty cuddles and looked from me over to the pasture at his new friend. "Sorry, little guy. It's not safe for you to hang out alone with her and we need to get going. Maybe we'll visit again later."

Who knew Lucky would get so attached to other fur babies like Skye and Dale's dairy cow? Maybe getting him a little, furry sibling wasn't the worst idea. He possessed more of a canine pack mentality than a kitty loner personality. I couldn't remember a single time of Lucky hiding underneath a couch or bed, cowering from people.

"Do you always talk to your cat like he's a person to reason with?" asked Wesley. I felt like the answer to that was obvious and ignored his question. He'd heard me reasoning with Lucky multiple times over the last few months.

"You already know the answer to that. What you should be doing is describing the guy that Dale saw outside Frosted," I said. "I bet the killer and the person Dale saw are one and the same so it's possible I saw them, too. I might know who the killer is if you tell me what Dale told you."

Wesley rubbed his chin, contemplating new ways to get me out of his investigation but he knew I was right. Without Dale, I was the only other person who might've noticed someone out of place at Frosted.

"Let's not jump to any conclusions. Dale said he saw a

medium-sized man that had dark hair, which pretty much describes the entire male population in Clover Creek, including me," Wesley replied. "That's why we asked a sketch artist to work with him."

That was unfortunate. "Anything else, like tattoos, scars, piercings, or maybe a wedding ring?" I asked.

"You don't think I already asked him that?" asked Wesley, looking at me over his notepad.

"What about his clothing? Did he seem rich, poor, outdoorsy? Was he dressed like a construction worker, a police officer, a cowboy, a military guy?" I asked.

"You just described the men from that 1970s band, The Village People," said Wesley. "And no, he didn't recall anything about his clothes. Said it might have been a suit or khakis but he couldn't remember."

Wesley flipped his notepad shut and opened my car door for me. "As always, Decker, thank you for somehow being the only citizen in all of Clover Creek to keep stumbling upon dead bodies. We appreciate your good samaritan services," he said.

"You make it sound like I do this on purpose," I said, strapping my seatbelt on.

"You make it sound like you don't," said Wesley.

12

Even though protocol dictated that I thank Marcus with a phone call or in-person with some cupcakes, I decided to go with the texting option.

Me: *Wow - thanks for the car save. That was amazing. I totally owe you.*

Marcus: *My pleasure - It's been a while since I worked on a car so it was a nice distraction from SmartWatches.*

Me: *You repaired it yourself?*

Marcus: *Definitely. I'm a huge car buff. Have any other cars that need repairing?*

Me: *Actually, I inherited a car that I can't identify. Maybe you could take a look at it sometime?*

Marcus: *How about tonight? I'll bring dinner over.*

That escalated pretty fast. I didn't know how I felt about seeing him again so soon.

Me: *Possibly. Let me get back to you.*

Marcus: *I have some new theories on the diamond ring theft - we could work on that together, too.*

Ohhh! He knew exactly how to push my buttons. He

had some good ideas for the last murder investigation we worked on. It couldn't hurt to get another perspective.

Me: *How does 6 PM at my place tonight sound?*

Marcus: *Works for me - see you then!*

After Lucky and I enjoyed an extra long, hot shower, I headed out to the Warehouse District to meet up with Shelby's psychic, Madame Omega. I still had a couple hours before reconvening with Shelby at six PM and I sensed Madame Omega knew more than she was letting on. Not a chance she predicted the ring would go missing when Tyler hadn't even decided until the last minute to propose.

The Warehouse District was known as the furniture store area during the day but a night-time fun area in the evenings. Nightclubs and bars were strategically placed at each end of the block or in furniture stores that had gone out of business. Even though it was daytime, I always felt a little underdressed for this part of town.

Shorts and a tee shirt were about as fancy as my attire went in the summer. And forget about wearing heels. At five-foot-eleven, flip-flops already gave me an extra centimeter of height than I needed.

"Come on, Lucky," I said, urging him to pick up the pace. I was starting to sweat, which wasn't a pretty look on me. My wavy hair became a face-clinging mash of mismatched curls and my amateur attempts at eyeliner were melting rapidly. I hoped Madame Omega's place was air-conditioned.

I gave the cat leash a gentle tug. It was too hot out to carry Lucky around in his kitty bjorn on my chest and considering his new fascination with finding a fur friend, he couldn't be trusted to heel. I harnessed him up and put him on a leash.

Who said cats preferred staying indoors? Lucky was beyond excited to stop and smell everything we passed. I only parked two blocks away but it took us a good twenty minutes to get to our destination.

Madame Omega's shop was right between the Velvet Emporium and the pretzel stand on the eastern edge of the block. Graffiti filled the walls of each building in the alley between them and a park bench stood right outside.

I peeked in through the window. It was packed. Surely, everyone had somewhere else they'd rather be? I couldn't believe how many people were there on a Sunday afternoon. Visiting a psychic wasn't the hugest waste of time but it was right up there with reading tabloid magazines. Entertaining but fake news.

On the plus side, I was blasted by cool arctic air when I stepped inside. The receptionist said everyone was there for a family reunion seance but was on their way out and asked me to come back in five minutes. I bought a pretzel with cheese while I waited and tried to think cool thoughts under the blistering sun. I was no psychic but I definitely saw another shower in my future.

After everyone filed out of the lobby, I entered. I wasn't sure what to expect but Madame Omega was an ambiance genius. First, I got a huge whiff of eucalyptus incense when I stepped into the back. It smelled like a combination of a spa and a nightclub. Second, hanging beads replaced the doors and tons of feathers and witchy knick-knack items were positioned everywhere. Threaded throughout were Kira's Gorgeous Green signature rainbow colored succulents with her branded silver ceramic pots.

Lucky was in kitty heaven with all the new scents and especially the plethora of feathers. The receptionist ushered me into the secret backroom, which contained a glowing crystal ball, purple silk curtains, candles, and smoke that came out of the vents.

Madame Omega was totally decked out like it was

Halloween. She had a crazy-patterned scarf wrapped around her head with a trailing veil that descended down her back. It looked like she put Claire's Accessories out of business with all the costume jewelry she wore.

"Hi, Madame Omega, I'm Ava, Shelby's friend and I was hoping to ask you some questions about---" I said before Madame Omega silenced me with her hand.

"I already know what your question is," she said. "And the answer is yes. You will die a lonely spinster if you continue down this path of denial."

"Denial? Of what?" I asked.

"Denial that you have a boyfriend," she said. She held out her arm and indicated for me to sit in the chair opposite the crystal ball.

"But I don't have a boyfriend," I said, taking a seat. How many times would I have to keep explaining that to everyone? Shelby must've said something to her about Marcus.

"So you're trying to deny that you're denying you have a boyfriend even though you just denied it?" asked Madame Omega.

"No. Wait, what? That wasn't my question. I'm here about my friend, Shelby's diamond engagement ring that you predicted would be stolen," I said, more than happy to change the subject.

"Yes, I know," she said, taking a seat opposite me, behind her crystal ball.

"Then why did you go on and on about my love life?" I asked. (Or rather, the lack thereof).

"The engagement ring was stolen on your watch because you don't believe in love," she said.

"That's silly and completely untrue," I said. Clover Creek was a small town. After Tessa's Channel Five news coverage of my disastrous mishap when I was jilted at the altar back in San Diego earlier this year and the live confrontation with my ex afterward, I assumed everyone considered me bad luck in the romance department. No clairvoyant skills required for that one! "Did Shelby tell you to say that?" Or maybe it was Kira when she bought the succulent plants from her.

"A woman who takes her cat with her everywhere is telling the world she is not interested in dating or romantic love of any kind," she said, pointing to Lucky.

"He gets scared when he's left at home alone," I said, picking him up and hugging him to my chest. The cold air was actually starting to make me a little chilly now that I'd gotten used to it.

"Well, he is very cute," she said, reaching out to pet him. "Better company than some of my exes so maybe you have something there with the cat."

"Did you talk to Tyler? How did you know he was going to propose?" I asked, redirecting her back to the engagement ring. I placed Lucky on top of the table so he could check it out.

"I'm a psychic. I know lots of things," she said.

I didn't have time for this. I needed to figure out what she knew. I stood up and leaned over the crystal ball. "If you don't tell me right now how you knew that engagement ring would go missing then I'm going to the police and telling them to add you to their suspect list," I announced in my sternest and most menacing voice possible.

She grabbed both of my hands in her own, throwing her back into her chair like someone just pushed her. A big swoosh of air flowed into the room. I could feel it coming from the overhead vent so I suspected Madame Omega had a button on the floor she controlled with her foot. She arched her back and resumed sitting straight as she said, "The spirits tell me that as soon as you believe in love again, the diamond ring will reappear."

13

I made it home just as a massive summer thunderstorm started. I texted Shelby to come by at five-thirty since Marcus was expected at six. I left the garage door open so she could avoid the rain. The nice part about inheriting a mansion, aside from simply inheriting a mansion, was that it came with a huge, ten-car garage so there were plenty of parking spots. Not that I ever planned to use them. I still hadn't even gotten around to buying a car of my own but it did provide a ton of storage space.

Skye and Lucky were overjoyed to be reunited again and began chasing each other around the garage. While they had fun, I brought Shelby up to speed on my day.

"Whoa, that's crazy and so sad. This whole engagement is cursed. I, for sure, can't marry Tyler now," she said.

"Let's not jump to any conclusions. All we know is that someone murdered Dale. It could've had absolutely nothing to do with the ring," I replied, even though I didn't believe it for a second. "What about Melanie?" I asked, changing the subject. "Did she tell anyone else about the ring?"

Shelby shook her head no. "She's a paralegal and keeps everything confidential, so no."

"And you're quite certain that she would have no reason to steal it?" I asked. I hoped the police already explored that angle. I made a mental note to ask Wesley where he stood with investigating Melanie. But otherwise, between that, Dale and Madame Omega, we were back to square one.

"I'm not certain of anything at this point but I'm especially confused about why you're driving your parents' old SUV when you have this fancy looking race car sitting in your garage?" asked Shelby, doing a double walk around of it.

"It's not very kitty friendly and I'm not even sure that I technically own it," I said.

"Then who does?" asked Shelby, trailing her fingers along its smooth, cherry red edges.

"Beats me. It was included with the house when I inherited it but I can't find any paperwork on it," I said, still somewhat repelled by how flashy it was.

"Tyler can help you with that. Wasn't it his office that handled the inheritance?" she asked.

"Yes, but his sister didn't exactly include the correct paperwork with that whole coverup scheme she had going on," I said. The entire inheritance became a big mess with all the false documentation Tyler's sister created to frame me for murder. I was grateful I still had the house and the bakery. I didn't want to push my luck by tracking down the real owner of that fancy sports car I had no urge to drive. I asked Tyler about it a while ago but he scoured Wendy's office and laptop and found nothing so I just left it at that.

"Why didn't you ask me?" she asked, looking more than offended. "I'm a librarian. Research is my middle name," said Shelby, snapping a ton of pictures of the car with her phone. "I'll look into it first thing tomorrow morning when I go to work. The library has special resources and access to different information you can't find online."

I hadn't used the library for research since high school. The one perk to choosing accounting as my major was not having to write research reports.

I was about to tell her that Marcus offered to help me with it but she was already inside the car, poking around.

"Hey, look," she said, pointing to the inside panel of the door and the front windshield. "The VIN is missing. I'm not an expert but I do know that every car is required to insert a VIN here, on the front windshield, as well as on the engine block."

"How do you know so much about cars?" I asked.

"Tyler is a huge car fanatic. It's the only reason he even works, so he can add to his car collection. You should see his garage," said Shelby. "I think he purchased all ten of his last cars from Grant directly. He used to give him a special deal." She used air quotes for the words *special deal*.

I knew nothing about lawyer salaries or car prices but if Tyler could afford a one hundred-thousand-dollar ring, a garage filled with designer cars should have been no problem. "My friend, Ruby's insurance company took a huge hit with all the fake insurance claims Grant was submitting for the cars." She didn't even bother filing a police report. Two consecutive life sentences for murdering his sister and Tyler's sister meant Grant wasn't getting out anytime soon.

"If this house belonged to Grant's sister, whom he killed, and he had it cleaned for you before he handed you the keys, I bet the car is his. He could've put it here after his sister died," said Shelby. That was a very plausible scenario. I was so preoccupied trying to clear my name from the murder suspect list, I didn't give the car much thought.

"That's a definite possibility," I agreed.

"Does it even run?" asked Shelby, pushing some of the control knobs and doohickies inside.

"That's a good question. Let me go grab the key fob. Ruby found it yesterday," I said, running back inside, up to my bedroom nightstand where Ruby left it the other morning.

I returned to the garage and handed her the key. "It's not starting. Maybe it's dead," Shelby said, handing the key fob back to me.

"Maybe it's a dud," I said. Only I would inherit a fancy, inoperable sports car.

"Why don't you ask Grant where the car came from?" asked Shelby. "I bet he doesn't even know you have it. He probably thinks the police confiscated it when they shut down his dealership."

That was another real possibility. He was locked up and sentenced right away. There was no chance the FBI would've allowed him to do an inventory audit of all the stolen cars that were seized. Because the cars were shipped via international cargo from Italy, the FBI had jurisdiction over them, not the local Clover Creek police.

I guessed I could write him a letter or postcard asking where the car came from, on the off and extremely remote chance it was legit and not stolen. "I doubt he'd respond to a letter. I'm the person who helped put him away," I said. Still, prison had to be pretty boring, so maybe he would respond.

"I meant, go to the prison and ask him in person," she said.

"How?" I asked. Didn't I need Grant's permission to be added to his visitor list? Something I seriously doubted he'd give me.

"Well, you're practically family considering you inherited his sister's house and bakery. I bet Wesley could help you get in to see Grant," said Shelby. Wesley used to date Shelby's original roommate, Brittany Westerheide, so she was more than familiar with Wesley and my relationship with him.

"You mean the cop that keeps telling me to mind my own business and not investigate Dale's murder or the missing diamond ring?" I asked.

"Neither of which you're doing. Technically, you're just looking into a parked car that's sitting in your garage with no VIN number. What's the harm in that? If anything, he should be happy that you're focusing your time and energy on something else," said Shelby. "Call him now."

"Why don't I wait until tomorrow? He's still pretty annoyed that I was the one who found Dale's body. I might want to wait at least twenty-four hours for that to subside," I said, give or take a few. I decided to pack some spirulina smoothies and drop by the precinct around his lunchtime. I wanted to reserve the morning for visiting Chloe, Wesley's cousin and the original person who installed the wall safe and security system at Frosted. I was hoping she would come by to take a look at the safe and see if she could figure out how someone managed to open it.

"Fine, but by this time tomorrow, you'd better be included on that prisoner visitor list," said Shelby, cracking the whip.

"All right. Then by this time tomorrow, you'd better have a good list of potential original owners of this car," I said.

She started crawling around on her knees.

"What are you doing?" I asked, kneeling down and trying to see what she was looking at.

"Looking for anything out of the ordinary that might help us identify the car," she said.

Lucky and Skye thought she was playing a game and

started doing the exact same thing on the other side of the car. They each slowly stalked her, attempting to take cover behind the wheels, and then darting out over the top, tagging her with their cute, little kitty paws before retreating quickly to the other side.

"Lucky and Skye think you're playing peek-a-boo with the car tires," I said, kneeling down and scooping up Skye for a quick kitty cuddle. She was even softer than I remembered. It almost made me sad I didn't have two cats, even if it fated me to a lonely life of spinsterhood.

Shelby held her outstretched arms for Lucky to jump into. He happily hopped onto her chest and gave her a proper puppy dog hello, licking all over her face.

"All right let's see if the VIN is hiding in here," she said, setting Lucky down and popping the front hood before peering into the engine. I joined her and leaned in. The interior was immaculate since it had never been driven, at least not by me.

"What are we looking for?" asked Marcus, flanking Shelby while peering into the engine.

Shelby and I both screamed in surprise before jumping up and hitting our heads on the roof of the car hood.

"Are you okay? I didn't mean to scare you. I saw the garage door open and figured you left it open for me since it's raining so hard outside and then I saw you both looking over here and joined you," he said.

Between the pouring rain, crackling thunder and the echo effect from the high ceilings, neither of us heard Marcus drive in. Lucky was totally unfazed and had already climbed up Marcus's leg to be held in the crook of his arm.

"You just surprised us, that's all. I didn't realize it was already six. I don't think you two have met before," I said, looking between Shelby and Marcus. They knew about each other but with Marcus's busy travel schedule, they never officially met in person. I retrieved Lucky from Marcus.

"Hi there, I'm Marcus Palmer," he said, extending his hand out to Shelby.

Shelby was rubbing her ostensibly bruised head with one hand and shook Marcus's hand with the other. Then realization dawned on her. She snapped her fingers and pointed at him. "You're that tech billionaire genius that Ava has a crush on and always talks about! Oops. Did I say that out loud? Sometimes I talk faster than I think. Forget I said that. How do they put it on those legal shows? Oh, right. The jury will strike my last statement."

I groaned and hid my face behind Lucky's. At least, I tried to. That was the problem with having a tiny, little four-pound kitten when you were five-foot-eleven. Not a whole lot of kitten to hide behind. Now, I understood the appeal of big, fluffy dogs. Maybe I should consider adopting a Doberman or one of those big dogs that carries a small keg of brandy on its collar that you see in cartoons.

Since there was no massive asteroid headed toward the garage at any moment, or anything else to save me from my current state of mortifying embarrassment, I cleared my throat as loud as I could and changed the subject.

"You remember Shelby. She's the one whose engagement ring was stolen before she even had a chance to see it," I said.

Either sensing my misery or simply being a gentleman, Marcus completely ignored Shelby's outburst and carried on as if it never happened, which was fine by me.

"And you think it might be in this car?" asked Marcus.

"No, this is the car I told you about before, the one that I have no information on. Shelby was helping me search for a VIN," I replied.

"You're in luck. I know exactly what kind of car this is," said Marcus, sliding into the driver's seat and fiddling with the controls and gadgets inside.

"You do?" Shelby and I both asked in unison.

"It's an Aston Martin Valkyrie. It's barely street legal," he said. "The prototype was intended for Formula One racing. They don't go into production until next year. It's worth about three million dollars," he said.

"No way! Too bad this one is broken. I can't get it to start," I said, handing the key fob to Marcus.

After pressing a couple pedals and pushing the key fob into the center, the engine hummed to life for Marcus. I jumped into the passenger side. "So you stick the key in like a CD?" I asked.

"That and you need to push your foot on the clutch and the brake in a manual transmission before hitting the start button, which is right here," he said, pointing to a button on the dashboard that swallowed the key.

"No wonder Ava is so smitten with you. You really are a genius," said Shelby. "Ugh. I did it again, didn't I? I said that out loud when really, I just meant to say it in my head. Just disregard that and strike it from the record."

Marcus chuckled and I found myself again wishing for a crashing asteroid to head our way.

"Thanks for the accolades but in this case, they're undeserved," he said, switching the engine off. "I'd love to credit my superior intellect in allowing me to decipher this car's inner workings but I have one of these back in Palo Alto."

Of course, he did. Why buy an economy hybrid when you could own a three million-dollar sports car?

"I think this one might actually be stolen," I said.

"Oh, yes, this car is most definitely stolen," said Marcus with a small chuckle.

I gasped with a sharp intake of air, followed by a weak,

squeaky noise. "Are you sure?" I asked. He looked at it for a grand total of maybe five minutes, if that.

"Oh, quite certain. There were only two Valkyrie prototypes made this year. One for the next James Bond movie and another for the Geneva Motor Show. I have the one from the showroom floor sitting in my garage back in Palo Alto and the second one vanished from the factory before it could be detailed. That's why there are no identifying marks on it, like a VIN or WIN," said Marcus.

"Is there any chance Palmer Tech can install a self-destruct button on this car to keep me out of prison?" I asked, trying to lighten the mood.

Shelby gave me a weird look.

"What? He's like Q from James Bond. He designs gadgets. Every car double-oh-seven was blown up when he was done with it," I said. "And grand theft auto is a Class B felony in Maine, which comes with a ten-year sentence." I'd been researching it ever since I suspected the car was stolen.

"In that case, maybe should we wipe our fingerprints off the car first," said Shelby.

14

After hitting *snooze* a gazillion times, I finally woke up from my Salted Caramel Cheesecake-induced dessert coma hangover. Marcus brought enough takeout food for ten people. He wasn't sure what I'd like so he chose every entree on the menu, along with extra generous servings of cheesecake, which Shelby and I happily indulged in.

We threw different theories around but our diamond ring pow-wow last night did nothing to shed more light on who might've stolen the car, nor who might've killed Dale, but at least, the mystery of the fancy sports car I'd been harboring was finally solved. Marcus was friends with the CEO at Aston Martin and promised to make a call on my behalf this morning to return the car without landing me behind bars. Now, I understood why wealthy people never went to jail. They were all friends with each other.

Ten AM I was too late to help open Frosted. On the plus side, I could not fire myself. On the downside, this would be the umpteenth time I was too late to help Caitlin, my new baking assistant.

"Come on, Lucky, wake up," I said, pulling the sheets off him. I'd never been a morning person but having a soft, cuddly kitten that also enjoyed sleeping in made it easier to hit the *snooze* button. "We're late, little buddy."

I tried nudging him awake but there was no response. If he didn't do this every morning, I might've been worried. I scooped him up and gently placed him in his kitty carrier.

I skipped straightening my hair and putting on makeup so I'd only be ninety minutes instead of two hours late. However, I completely forgot to consider the summertime construction. One problem with living in small towns was the total lack of alternate routes. It was almost noon by the time I breezed in the back door of Frosted.

Lucky was fully awake by the time we got there and ready for his breakfast.

"I am so sorry I'm late!" I said to Caitlin who not only completed all of the baking for the day but also cleaned up the kitchen and was waiting for customers at the register.

I could never get sick of the aroma of freshly baked cupcakes in the morning. I took a huge whiff as I made my way to the front room where I poured Lucky his morning kitty cream.

"Don't worry, I did everything already," Caitlin replied, arranging the last of the cupcakes on the display counter. Unlike me, Caitlin was graced with an amazing head of blonde hair. She had loose, beachy waves that cascaded around her face perfectly.

"You're a lifesaver. Remind me to give you a raise once we start making more money," I told her with a grateful smile. "In the meantime, can I at least make you one of my famous iced tiramisu lattes?"

I pulled the whole milk from under the counter and felt a sad twinge for Dale.

"Sure, but you don't have to. Finding time to study in

between customers has been a huge help," she said, pulling out her college textbooks and flopping them onto the counter. Caitlin was pre-med. She planned to become a brain surgeon.

In the meantime, she was an excellent baker. Her mother was the star of a big YouTube baking channel and she taught Caitlin everything she knew, which was the reason I hired her.

"Did you ever talk to Dale the Dairy Farmer when he brought the deliveries in?" I asked, filling the first metal cup with milk.

"All the time. He was such a nice guy. I heard you were the one that found him. That must've been terrible," she said, putting her highlighter down.

"Yes, it was. Do you know anyone who might've wanted to hurt Dale?" I asked, hitting the steam wand a few times to warm it up.

"Everyone loved Dale. Everyone that knew him, that is. He was pretty shy and mostly kept to himself. But maybe one of his secrets got him killed," said Caitlin with a conspiratorial rise of her eyebrow.

"Secrets? What secrets?" I asked, steaming the first batch of milk.

"Everyone has secrets. The exterior shell that you present to the world and want everyone to see is often unlike the real you who is secretly hiding on the inside," said Caitlin with a knowing nod.

"Let me guess, you're taking Psychology 101 this summer?" I asked, glancing over at her textbook: *The Human Within.*

"Yes, how did you know?" she asked before looking down at her books. "Right. Well, it doesn't take a college course to know that people don't always tell the whole truth."

"I'm pretty open and have no secrets," I said, mixing in the tiramisu syrup and pouring her latte over ice.

"The entire town knows that you're secretly dating that tech billionaire genius, Marcus Palmer," she said with a dreamy smile. "Although if he were my boyfriend, I'd make sure the whole world knew it."

"He's not my boyfriend," I said, handing her drink to her.

She winked at me. "Sure, he isn't."

"Is this a private party or can I join in, too?" asked Kira, coming through the front door in a man's suit and tie.

"If it is a party, we're underdressed," I said, looking from her to Caitlin.

"I remember that costume," said Caitlin, passing her latte to Kira.

"Are you off to rehearsal?" I asked, handing the second latte to Caitlin and making a third latte for myself.

"Yes and no. Today, I'm standing in for another actor who's stuck at work," said Kira, sucking down a huge gulp of her iced latte. "Mmm! This tastes like a specialty ice cream dessert."

"It's a tiramisu latte. Do you like it?" I asked, shaking mine with some ice.

"Definitely! And I bet it pairs well with a Strawberry Filled Tiramisu Cupcake with Mascarpone Buttercream Frosting?" said Kira, pointing to one in the display case.

"For sure," said Caitlin, handing her a cupcake. "Thanks so much for being so supportive when I quit the play for summer school,"

"Of course, education is important and we girls need to stick together," said Kira, tapping on Caitlin's textbook while giving me a knowing smile.

"Yes, women helping women," I sang, half-mocking Kira who was really only helping herself. The fact that

Caitlin benefited was simply an unintended by-product of Kira's actions.

"How about helping me some more by sewing these pockets shut?" asked Kira, looking at me. She handed me the pants which looked like they'd seen better days. There was potting soil and some grass clinging to the bottom. It looked like Kira wore these in her shop. I shook them out over the trash bin.

"Why would you want to sew the pockets shut?" asked Caitlin, taking another sip of her tiramisu latte.

"To hide stuff," said Kira.

"Like what?" asked Caitlin.

"Like my super wide hips. Open pockets make them look even larger than they already are. But flat pockets are very slimming and flattering. So I sew mine shut. It allows me to eat more of these without consequences," said Kira, pointing to her cupcake.

"Sure, come on back. I still have the sewing kit here from last week," I said, popping a straw in my latte and taking it with me. "Didn't I just sew these exact same pants last Friday?"

Theatre clothes all looked alike to me but I remembered their distinctly strong mothball scent. Community theatre costumes didn't get a lot of wear and sat in boxes for years at a time so they smelled like it, too.

"Yeah, I accidentally left something in the pocket last time and had to rip it open. Sorry," she said, with a big smile.

That actually made it easier. The same color thread from before was still in the needle. It only took me five minutes to sew it back up.

After the barista arrived to help Caitlin out for the day, I packed some Strawberry Filled Tiramisu Cupcakes with Mascarpone Buttercream Frosting into a box and headed out to Goldie Locks. That was where Wesley's cousin, Chloe was apprenticing as a locksmith. Thankfully, it was also within walking distance of Frosted so I could avoid the construction traffic. Once the trolley was built, I hoped it would have air conditioning. The outdoor summer heat hit me like a furnace.

I didn't want to waste time while Lucky smelled every cubic meter between here and the locksmith so I strapped him into his kitty bjorn.

"Hi, Goldie, I brought some cupcakes for you and Chloe," I announced upon entering, waving my box like a peace offering. Goldie wasn't big on visitors unless they were paying customers. I discovered that when Chloe first started working here and Goldie practically kicked me out at gunpoint when she discovered I'd only come by to socialize.

"Chloe's not here and carbs are evil," she said, pointing to the door.

Perhaps I should've brought a healthy green smoothie instead. It was difficult to know when to bring a spirulina smoothie or cupcakes. They were such very different people.

"Do you know where I can find her?" I asked, scooping my cupcakes right off the counter before they were smashed and thrown into the trash.

"Why? So you can interrupt her work and ruin her productivity?" she asked.

That pretty much summed up what Goldie thought about socializing and friendship. She was more like a drill sergeant than a local, small-town locksmith.

"There was a problem with my safe at the bakery. Well, not exactly a problem," I immediately corrected myself. I didn't want to make it sound like Chloe was incompetent since she was my friend. "More like a user error. I'm not sure how to operate it and might need a refresher course."

Goldie eyed me suspiciously. "We don't do refresher courses. You'll have to pay or ask Chloe to do it on her own time."

Fair enough. "Great. Is she around?"

"She's at another job all day. You can come by tomorrow," she said with a dismissive wave of her hand as she headed to the back of the shop.

I glanced at the whiteboard behind the counter and saw their schedule on it. It read *Whitmore Savings and Loan* as the only appointment of the day. That had to be where Chloe was.

Whitmore Savings and Loan was the biggest and pretty much the only bank in Clover Creek. Everyone preferred the ambiance of local smaller banks and credit unions. After a huge scandal when a national bank chain in Clover Creek opened up tons of fake accounts and falsified millions of credit card applications with their customer's information, no one trusted big banks anymore.

Whitmore was in Town Square, only a couple blocks from Frosted. For sure, someone there would appreciate my cupcakes. And they did. I was greeted with a warm welcome and grateful smiles from the entire staff who not only ate my Strawberry Filled Tiramisu Cupcakes with Mascarpone Buttercream Frosting but did so happily. Frosted's business account was here as well as my personal account. I'd been banking here ever since my dad gave me my first piggy bank as a kid.

I made a deposit while I was here. The teller was eating one of my cupcakes. She looked from the deposit slip to the cupcake box name. "Oh, you're the stuffed cupcake lady! Did you make these?" she asked.

"Sure did. Do you like them?" I asked.

"No, I *love* them. You're a genius. I no longer have to choose between my two favorites. I can enjoy both a tiramisu and a cupcake all wrapped into one," she said, picking it up and taking another bite.

"I'm so glad you like them. It's a new dessert cupcake I'm trying out," I said.

She winked at me. "Well, it definitely works for me." She handed me back a deposit slip. "Is there anything else I can help you with?"

"I was looking for Chloe Lockwood. I heard she was working onsite here today," I said.

She leaned in and whispered. "She's like a bank vault magician. We're all in awe of her. Mr. Whitmore had to order a new vault after she broke into it in less than five minutes and bypassed all of our alarm triggers. She's doing a walk around now, looking for other security holes that need to be plugged," she said, pointing to the back of the bank.

"Thanks, I'll go find her," I said.

"I'm not sure if you're supposed to be back there unescorted. It's limited to bank employees only," she said.

I held up my other box of cupcakes. "I was just going to drop off some French Vanilla Cheesecake Filled Cupcakes for her," I said, lifting the box open to let the aroma waft over to her.

"Did you want one? I'm sure Chloe wouldn't mind sharing," I said.

"You're definitely bribing the right girl. I cannot say no to your stuffed cupcakes. I'll walk you back there," she said. She locked up her drawer, pulled the shade down on her window to mark it closed, and met me on the other side. I handed her a cupcake as we walked around the corner to the back. "Whoa. I can't believe I like this one equally as much as the other one. What is it?"

"I'm so glad you like both of them. This is another new flavor I'm trying out, French Vanilla Cheesecake Filled Cupcakes. They pair perfectly with the Mexican Mocha Lattes at Frosted," I said.

She moaned in appreciation. "I'll remember to order that next time I visit."

"Ava? I thought I smelled cupcakes," said Chloe, coming around the corner.

"I'll leave you with Chloe," said the teller with a smile. "You'll make sure she gets out, okay? She's not really supposed to be back here."

I passed the teller another cupcake when I saw her wavering about leaving me here. "One for the road?" I asked.

"For sure!" she said, grabbing a second one with her other hand.

Chloe was one of Lucky's favorite kitty sitters in the entire world. She actually catsat Lucky before I even adopted him. He woke up from his slumber and sprang from his kitty bjorn into her arms. The face licking started immediately, followed by the tail wagging and the loud kitty meows of excitement.

"It's my favorite little, ruddy Abyssinian. How did you get so big?" she asked, nuzzling him against her neck. I almost corrected her that he really wasn't that big but technically, she hadn't seen him in a couple months so he probably did gain a pound since then, a twenty-five percent increase in size.

Chloe pulled out a string with a small rubber ball at the end and threw it down the hallway for Lucky to fetch.

"Do you always carry that around just in case you run

into a cat that enjoys playing fetch?" I asked. That was Lucky's favorite toy. She made one for the house and one for the bakery just for Lucky.

"I got bored and made it with the string they use in the vault to tie the money bands together after they're done counting it," she said, pulling a couple more Lucky fetch toys out of her pocket and handing them over to me.

"Bored?" I asked. I had no idea they used string in bank vaults, but then again, I'd never been surrounded by that much money before.

"Yes, I completed my walk through over an hour ago. Mr. Whitmore thought it would take me longer so I've been waiting for him to get out of his meeting in order to brief him on my findings. Then I smelled your cupcakes and came out here," she said. "I figured I'd give these to you whenever I saw you next."

"I actually came here to find you," I replied, depositing Lucky's fetch toys into my purse.

"Me, why?" she asked.

Lucky fetched his toy back and Chloe threw it again. While they continued to play, I brought her up to speed on what happened with Shelby's missing diamond engagement ring.

"Wesley already asked me about it," she said. "It's completely impenetrable, just like the one in your home bedroom," she said.

That one was already installed and locked when I inherited the house. The second one at the bakery was purchased by the former owner but she never got around to installing it. They weren't returnable and much too heavy to resell on eBay. The shipping cost alone would've been ten times what the safe cost. Chloe needed the practice so she offered to install it at the bakery for me. It wasn't until Tyler gave me the diamond engagement ring that I actually used it for anything.

"But somehow, someone must've gotten in there and stolen it," I said.

"Impossible. It's a special order von Bursten fortress safe. It self-destructs everything inside if there is tampering of any kind," she said. "Unless, of course, you're a trained expert, like me."

"Is there a clone of you in Clover Creek that can crack these types of safes?" I asked, picking up Lucky's fetch toy and throwing it down the hall. "This is the last time, Lucky."

"Doubtful. Even Goldie can't open one of those locks without setting off the fire failsafe. You're certain that it didn't self-destruct?" she asked.

Before I could answer, Lucky was demanding our attention again. How could he already be back? There were little kitty scratches at my ankles, prompting me to continue playing fetch. I ignored him and answered Chloe instead.

"You mean, did I fail to notice a huge fire in my kitchen while someone tried to break into the safe?" I asked.

Before Chloe had a chance to respond with her own witty remark or scoff at my sarcasm, a small fire went off at our feet, followed by a short, explosive sound and a cloud of purple dye spraying us from everywhere. Purple smoke filled up the hallway and burned my lungs.

"Lucky!" I called out. "Where are you?"

Lucky found me, crawling his way up my leg before cowering in his kitty bjorn. I stepped away from the smoke and saw that he was covered in purple dye, too.

"What was that?" I asked between gasping for fresh air and trying to wipe the dye out of my eyes. I wanted to comfort Lucky but my hands were covered in purple ink. I'd just make it worse if I tried.

Chloe waved her arms around to dissipate the smoke. She picked up a stack of burnt, purple hundred-dollar bills. "It looks like Lucky fetched a dye pack instead of his toy. It's tied with the same string I used to make his fetch toys," she said. "They're preset to go off thirty seconds after passing the vault doors."

Too bad Tyler's diamond ring didn't have the same fail-safe on it.

15

After a lengthy apology to Mr. Whitmore, Chloe came back to the employee room where I was trying in vain to remove the purple dye.

"Why is this not coming off?" I asked, switching from a green scouring pad to steel wool.

Chloe ran over and grabbed it out of my hand. "Don't do that! You'll take your first, second, third and possibly fourth layer of skin off."

"Then how do we get it off? Is there a special soap or something?" I asked, looking around and under the sink.

"You can't get it off. You just have to wait for it to wear off on its own," she said, rinsing her arms in the sink.

"And how long will that take?" I asked, spraying my arms with a random bottle of Windex I found on the counter, hoping that might help.

"A couple weeks, give or take," said Chloe.

"A couple weeks!" I couldn't be purple for a couple weeks. "Why?" I whined, more to myself than anyone.

"That's the whole point. If you rob a bank, the police

can easily find you," said Chloe. "On the plus side, my skin now matches my new hair color."

Chloe was always changing her hair color from red to pink to blue to green. I wasn't even sure what her real hair color was but today it was purple. I wasn't as brave, nor could I look as great as Chloe did. She had one of those funky, super short, but chic and stylish bob cuts with sharp, angular lines that framed her face. At least, my hair was still in its non-stylish bun from earlier this morning and managed to avoid most of the purple dye.

"Well, I'm glad you're not mad about this. This is totally my fault for ignoring his fetch requests," I said. I could already hear Goldie reiterating what a big distraction I was. Goldie was right. I was certainly not a factor in making Chloe's day more productive.

"Who could be mad at the cutest kitty in the world?" said Chloe, reaching over and petting Lucky. He responded with a face rub on Chloe's hand, successfully smearing more purple dye across his little kitty cheek.

I wiped Lucky down as much as I could before we headed out of the bank. I was dying for a nice, hot, steamy shower but according to Mr. Whitmore, heat and steam were not the solution. They would only saturate the dye more by allowing it to seep into our pores. If Windex didn't work, maybe I could try some acetone nail polish remover. Lucky and I could swing by the Stop-N-Shop on the way home.

As we walked out the front doors of the bank, we were hit with a huge light streaming in our faces and multiple news cameras.

"Whoa, did you just try to rob Whitmore Savings and Loan?" asked Tessa, her blue eyes practically popping out as she scanned both me and Chloe with unmasked scrutiny.

Tessa was a classic frenemy. Sometimes, she was helpful, and sometimes she was most definitely not. This was one of the latter times. Being the Channel Five anchor for Ten Minutes With Tessa, she liked covering scandalous stories to shock people and increase her ratings. Her most popular episodes to date were the ones where she accused me of murder on live TV.

"No, of course not," I said, knowing it certainly looked like we did.

"Then why are you both covered in purple dye?" she asked.

"Well, if you must know, there was a kitty fetch toy mishap with some of the dye pack money and well, you can see the result," I said, looking down at my arms and clothes that were now purple. I didn't even bother to look at myself in the mirror. After seeing the random purple blotches all over Chloe's face, I was too afraid. I might have to avoid mirrors for another month.

"Want to elaborate?" asked Tessa, throwing the mic back in front of me.

"Nope," I said, continuing to walk around her towards Frosted.

Undeterred, Tessa and her camera crew followed me. "Did you try to rob Whitmore Savings and Loan to pay for a good criminal defense lawyer after murdering your dairy vendor, Dale?"

Ugh. Tessa. She made it so hard to be her friend. The last time I saw her was almost two months ago when she helped spotlight Lucky's agility school on her show. The school's owner was so grateful, they finally let Lucky enroll there. Tessa also figured out that my long lost cousin, Sakara Decker, was the anonymous donor who allowed me to keep both Frosted and the house. Hence, my last memory of Tessa was a warm and fuzzy one. Now this. It was like we were back to square one on the first day I met her when she accused me of murdering my boss.

"I did not murder Dale. He was already dead when I got to his farm!" I snapped, simply reiterating what I'm sure the police already disclosed to her.

"But didn't you murder him to cover up another crime, a diamond theft from your best friend, Shelby, when you palmed her engagement ring, because you were so crazy jealous of her and wanted her to remain single forever, like you are?" brayed Tessa, pushing the mic back in my face.

Too bad I wasn't trying to rob the bank because I would've worn a ski mask, not only protecting my face from the purple dye but also from being recognized by Tessa. Before I could answer, police sirens sounded in the back.

Wesley pulled up to the curb and jumped out of his car. He took one look at Chloe and me before flashing his badge and ordering Tessa to leave.

"That's it. Show's over here," he said, pointing to Tessa's news van and camera crew.

"Are you in on the bank heist too? Trying to cover up for your cousin, Chloe, and helping her rob the bank?" asked Tessa, shoving the mic into Wesley's face, which turned bright red; but before he had a chance to respond, I shoved Wesley down the bank steps and back towards his police cruiser.

"Explain to me again why you're friends with Tessa," said Wesley as he threw the car into drive and sped off.

"What would the world be like without frenemies?" I asked. In Tessa's defense, we did look pretty guilty and shocking news was her thing. It wasn't as if she pretended to be a reporter who didn't go after the most controversial stories. That was who she was.

Kind of like me. I seemed to always find myself in questionable circumstances. This might be why Tessa and I were such good friends. My life gave her news anchor career the burning material it needed to keep thriving as the go-to gossip finder.

16

The nice part about having a police officer for a friend was that he knew exactly how to get the purple dye out. There was a special solvent at the police station, which was where we all went.

Wesley and Chloe's grandpa, whom everyone affectionately called Grandpa Lockwood, was a retired police officer who enjoyed manning the front desk. This would be the first time I'd ever seen Grandpa Lockwood without cupcakes in tow for him. His favorites were the Boston Creme filled ones that I decorated with little handcuffs, police batons, and police hats.

"Who's been playing with bank criminals?" asked Grandpa Lockwood.

Chloe and I ran up to hug him but he gave us the Heisman. "Why don't we save the hellos for after you both look a little less like Barney the Dinosaur?"

He directed us to the police locker room in the back. "There are two huge bottles of solvent in each of the showers. It won't get everything out but it should remove most of it so you'll just be a lighter shade of purple by the time you're done. Rub it in, let it sit for ten minutes and then scrub it off with those special sponges. There are some old police tee shirts and sweats sitting on the bench for you to change into when you're done."

"Does it work on cats, too?" I asked, holding Lucky up. Lucky was not at all happy about his current state of purple and still trying to lick it off. Fearing its toxicity, I tried to deter him from any more self-cleaning.

He shrugged. "I've never actually tried it on cats. But it does work on cat burglars," he laughed, cracking himself up at his own joke.

"Thanks, Grandpa Lockwood," we both chimed before heading into the locker room.

The solvent required a few ten-minute trials but an hour later, I was finally brave enough to look in the mirror. Lucky was simply a faded shade of light purple and so was I. In the right light, it almost looked like a tan. Or maybe a spray tan gone wrong with a blotchy effect.

"If you dye your hair purple, we could be twins," said Chloe, looking at our reflections in the mirror. Unlike her, I could never pull off purple hair. Plus, having an unruly mass of waves and curls, it was best not to draw any undue attention to it.

"Could these outfits land us a position on the force?" I asked Chloe, looking down at the shirts that said *Property of Clover Creek Police* that Grandpa Lockwood probably pulled from the reject pile of sample shirts the police department ordered.

"Doubtful. A costume party, possibly," she said. "Ready to go take a look at your impenetrable vault?"

"Sure," I said. Lucky's kitty bjorn was ruined. I simply dropped it into the waste can. Lucky jumped on the edge of the bin and tightrope-walked the rim, looking down at it and then at me. "Don't worry, little guy. We'll get you another one on the way home."

Chloe held out her arms and Lucky jumped into them. She carried him to Wesley's car, and he drove us to Frosted. We all piled out of the car and into the back room where Chloe started inspecting the safe. I had it installed at eye level. Ruby had to use a stool to get into it since she was only five-foot-four. Chloe had to do the same.

I had no idea what checking a safe entailed but Chloe locked it, unlocked it, and seemed to be looking for possible signs of tampering. She unscrewed the safe dial, checked the interior walls of the safe, along with the integrity of the walls surrounding it and then sighed before hopping off the stepladder and grabbing a cupcake from the inventory in the back.

"Well?" asked Wesley. "Was this an inside job?"

"Very funny," I said, punching Wesley in the shoulder.

"What? The cat might've done it. You know, cat burglars?" said Wesley, laughing at his own joke just like his grandfather.

"You so missed your calling as a stand-up comedian," I said.

As if sensing he'd been unjustly accused, Lucky latched onto Wesley's pant bottoms and growled. I reached down and pulled him into my arms. "It's okay, Lucky. Wesley didn't mean it. He's just really bad at telling jokes."

"Enough picking on your favorite detective," said Wesley, mocking a hurt look.

"Favorite detective?" I asked. Where did that come from?

"Aren't I?" asked Wesley, straightening his posture.

"Technically, you're the only detective in all of Clover Creek and the only one that I know; so sure, we can call you my favorite detective," I said. I resisted the urge to make a snarky remark since I did want to know what he found out from Melanie. I had a feeling she was hiding something. Or maybe I was just paranoid after Caitlin's declaration that everyone had secrets.

"I am so not referring to you as my favorite detective," said Chloe, crossing her arms and rolling her eyes.

"All right, all right. Enough picking on your cousin who saved you from public Channel Five news humiliation by rescuing you with my car. What can you tell us about the safe?" asked Wesley, redirecting his focus on Chloe.

"Yes, our hero. The optics on that looked great! Being hauled away on live TV in the back of a police cruiser after coming out of the bank, covered in purple dye," said Chloe with a sardonic smile. Not giving him a chance to respond, Chloe walked over to the safe and hopped up the stepladder. "There is nothing here to indicate that this lock was meddled with in any way."

Wesley threw his palms up and asked, "So it was an inside job. Decker stole the ring?"

"Or someone else who has the combination?" asked Chloe. "You did leave that instruction manual lying around your office before I installed it."

They both looked at me. "That was last February. It's June. Who would steal a safe combo number and then sit on it for four months on the off-chance of finding a one hundred thousand-dollar diamond in there someday?"

"Maybe they weren't sitting on it and they've been here every day, checking to see if there was anything worth stealing inside it," replied Chloe.

"I would've seen them on the cameras," I argued. Wesley gave me a disapproving look. "I only stopped paying for them a month ago."

Lucky ran up with his fuzzy red ball and dropped it at Wesley's feet to signal he wanted to play fetch again.

"You stopped paying?" asked Chloe. "I spent a lot of time hooking up that system."

"You know I have that huge credit card bill to pay off and Frosted is doing okay but only barely," I explained.

"But you have a free place to live," she said. That was true. I inherited my former boss's house and even if I hadn't, I could still live at home in my parents' house. It wasn't like they were there now that they'd embarked on a mission to try out every cruise ship in the world.

"Apparently, the former owner had a lot of back property taxes she hadn't paid in years and there was a lien on the place for the recent remodel she did. So yes, I did inherit a free place to live and all of the debt that came along with it," I said.

My parents would've easily given me the money but they'd already paid so much for my wedding that I felt terrible asking them for more. Especially when it was a house too large for me to really live in. Once that last lien was paid off, I could technically sell it, settle my credit card debt and still have enough left to buy another newer and much smaller house.

I just loved that house so much, I wasn't sure I could part with it even if I had to. I knew Grant never intended for me to have it forever and his sister, whom he killed, for sure never intended for me to have it, not at all. But it was home.

"Did you talk to Melanie, Tyler's paralegal? She was the only one that knew about the diamond ring," I said. Since the safe was a dead end, it was worth revisiting the suspect list.

"Yes, but she was out of town on Friday, unlike your friend, Ruby who conveniently flew back early," said Wesley.

"You know Ruby. She didn't do it," I said.

"And she's not the only one that knew the combination to the safe. I do, too," said Chloe. "You don't think I did it, do you?"

"What is this? Pick on Wesley day?" he asked.

"You know who else knows the combination to this safe?" asked Chloe. "Grant and his sister, the original owners. I had to wire all of Ava's inheritance paperwork to the safe company in order for them to share the lock code with me to open it."

"Nice try but his sister is dead so it's kind of doubtful she's our culprit and Grant's serving two consecutive life sentences up in Statesville," said Wesley.

"But maybe he sold the information to someone in prison. We should pay him a visit and ask. Or maybe the guards know something," I said. It wouldn't be beneath Grant to persuade someone to break into the safe periodically and check for cash or valuables.

"Fine. But you can't bring a cat into prison," he said.

"But isn't prison designed for cat burglars?" I said, giving Grant a wink and elbowing him in the side.

"I'll watch Lucky while the two of you torture each other with bad jokes on your way to prison," said Chloe, picking Lucky up and giving him a kiss.

I went over to the counter where Chloe was to grab my purse and say goodbye to Lucky. "Don't worry, Lucky. I'll be out soon with good behavior. If not, Uncle Wesley will steal a spoon from the prison chow hall and dig us out to freedom."

"So we're not even waiting until we're in the car to restart the bad jokes?" asked Wesley.

17

I've never been imprisoned, unless you counted being grounded in my room all through high school for breaking curfew because of my broken Mickey Mouse watch. Technically, I shouldn't have been blamed for that since my parents were the ones that provided said watch.

Statesville Penitentiary was nothing like my childhood bedroom. For one thing, there was metal everywhere, reinforced by even more metal instead of wainscoting and wood paneling. There were also tons of armed guards, attack dogs and rows of concrete pillars instead of rock star posters and stuffed animals. It was also the greyest place on earth, from the floors to the ceilings to the bars, unlike my bedroom, which featured various appealing shades of pink and purple. I went ahead of Wesley while he ran back out to his car to secure his gun and our phones. Apparently, we weren't allowed to bring anything inside the visiting room.

"Ma'am, you cannot bring those cupcakes into this facility. No baked goods of any kind," said the guard, who took my ID card and photocopied it. At barely one inch taller than my five-foot-eleven inches, his stature failed to intimidate me. But being called *ma'am* was pretty brutal. I wasn't even thirty yet.

"Can't you X-ray them for knives and the like?" I asked.

"Have you never heard of a ceramic gun? Anyone with a 3D printer could easily put one together and scatter the pieces into a box of cupcakes," said the guard.

"Couldn't you use a knife to poke around and check for pieces or other hidden things?" I asked. I made Grant's favorite flavor: Amaretto Apple Streusel Pie Cupcakes, which weren't easy to bake. I even ran out to the store to get fresh Granny Smith apples, but I did it because I hoped to convince Grant to speak to me or at the very least, not try to murder me again.

"Even if there were no physical items hidden inside them, they could be poisoned," he said, handing me back my license.

"What if I ate one to prove they're not poisoned?" I asked, returning my license to the wallet in my purse.

"You could have secretly taken an antidote before coming in here," he said. "I saw 'The Princess Bride.' I know what's up."

Jeez. Paranoid much? I wondered if they were still good so it might not even matter. Since we didn't have an appointment, they made us wait for almost four hours before we were allowed to go in. Wesley had to call his father, the Clover Creek Chief of Police to allow us to get that far. My cupcakes ordinarily held up well but they were usually kept inside a refrigerated display case, the temperature perfectly controlled for baked goods, not being subjected to a two-hour car ride with open windows since the driver refused to put on the AC to save gas, and winding up inside a stuffy prison reception waiting area.

"I told you they wouldn't allow you to bring those in

here," said Wesley, crossing his arms and nodding his solidarity with the world's most distrustful guard. "Hey, Joe. How's it going?" Then they did a weird, secret fraternity fist and shoulder-bump guy thing.

"Joe, meet Ava Decker. She's an over-zealous, over-curious, over-energetic neighborhood cupcake baker in Clover Creek and also the same person that helped us put Grant Donovan away two months ago," said Wesley. Joe smiled and shook my hand. "Ava, this is my good buddy, Joseph Bonetti. We went to the Police Academy together and Joe set the record for being the best shot, not only in our entire class but the whole history of the Academy. To this day, no one before or since has ever shot more bullseyes in a row."

"Wow, very impressive," I replied, stating the obvious. What I really wanted to know was: what kind of juicy dirt did he have on Wesley that I could use later? "So… have any good stories about Wesley?" I asked.

Joe gave me a knowing look and said, "I do, but it'll cost you."

"Are you asking for a bribe? Because I totally would since getting some good dirt on Wesley would be so worth whatever you're charging for it but I have to confess, I'm totally broke," I said.

"I was referring to the cupcakes," said Joe, motioning towards the box that apparently was never destined for Grant's cell.

"So basically, you're not ultra paranoid that I might've concealed an elaborately constructed device or sprinkled poison into these cupcakes, you just wanted them for yourself?" I asked. I knew a cupcake addict when I saw one.

"How about a compromise? You can have eleven and I'll just give one to the prisoner?" I asked, flipping the cupcake box lid open.

"Deal," he said while pulling out the visitor log for us to sign.

"Is that Tyler Roberts, the lawyer and Shelby's boyfriend?" I asked, looking at the names before us. Tyler Roberts was a pretty generic name. It could've been someone else entirely different but a Tyler Roberts visiting Grant Donovan? That was highly unlikely.

Wesley pulled the log closer for inspection and asked Joe some questions in code numbers. Joe typed a few things into his computer and flipped the screen around for us to see. It was definitely Shelby's Tyler Roberts.

"He's listed as Grant's lawyer," said Wesley.

"Why would he defend the person who murdered his sister? Is that even legal? It's definitely a conflict of interest and isn't he required to recuse himself from consulting his sister's killer?" I asked. I'd seen plenty of "Law & Order" episodes to know something about the courts.

"All good questions. Why don't we ask Grant ourselves?" suggested Wesley, signing his name into the log.

Not only was Grant super grateful for my Amaretto Apple Streusel Pie Cupcake, but he was also super chatty. Unfortunately, he had nothing pertinent to say about the safe, the missing diamond, or the mystery car in my garage.

Grant wasn't your typical criminal. A con artist and an extremely good looking one at that, prison only seemed to make him more handsome. Being chained to a prison desk that was bolted to the floor and dressed in all orange, he was still a looker. He flashed his signature flirty Hollywood smile at me from across the table.

"Ava, you are just as lovely as ever. And your cupcakes

are even more delicious than I remember," he said, taking a bite and savoring it. I couldn't believe he was the same man that pointed a gun at me just a few months ago and threatened to kill me.

"Thanks, I think," I said, unsure of the proper protocol for conversing with your previous wannabe murderer on a prison visit.

"To what do I owe the pleasure of this delightful visit from my favorite baker?" he asked. Wow, he was really pouring the charm on thick. Or was that sarcasm? I couldn't tell the difference.

"We want information about the safe you purchased for your sister at Frosted. Who else knew the combination? Did you tell anyone?" asked Wesley.

"I have no idea what you're talking about. What safe?" replied Grant, putting on his most innocent look. It was so good, even I believed him.

Wesley pushed a copy of the safe purchase receipt across the table so it was right in front of Grant. I gave it to him before we left Frosted. It had the Frosted Bakery as the delivery address and Grant's name at the top as the buyer.

"You know what would help jog my memory?" asked Grant, leaning forward as far as his handcuffs would allow. "How about weekly cupcake deliveries every Friday? At least a dozen to start."

"Not gonna happen, Grant," said Wesley before I could say yes. Murderer or not, I had to thank Grant's devious intervention that allowed me to inherit Frosted and that beautiful mansion I was too in love with to sell, despite being broke and really needing the money. I wanted to say yes. It seemed like a small price to pay to get the information I needed. "Tell us what we need to know at once or we're out of here."

Grant leaned back in his chair, putting on his most

debonair James Bond look of nonchalance. "Why don't you tell me what this is all about and maybe we can work out a deal? I bought my sister a lot of things, possibly the safe that you're referring to, but I don't remember it, much less, the safe combination numbers."

Grant didn't strike me as an overly generous brother who liked to lavish his half-sister with gifts, especially while plotting her murder. He was lying about something but I couldn't figure out what it could be. "And Tyler Roberts is your lawyer?" I asked.

"Hardly. He only said that so he could ask me about the same safe you seem so excited about," said Grant. "He's not my lawyer. It was the only way he could get on the visitor roster."

"Tyler already asked you about the safe?" I asked, giving Wesley a closer look. That was very odd and also highly suspicious. Tyler was about five-foot-ten, fitting the description of the man Dale said he saw hanging out in the back of Frosted. But why would Tyler steal his own ring?

"Maybe. How about our cupcake deal? Or better yet, why not take me to see this safe at Frosted and perhaps that might jog my memory," said Grant with a smile.

"I can have you locked up in solitary if you don't give us the answers that we're looking for," said Wesley, pounding his fist on the table.

"Go ahead. I'm not really into my roommates anyway," said Grant.

Clearly, Wesley's macho tough guy act wasn't going to work on someone as sophisticated as Grant.

"Did you give anyone the lock code to the safe?" I asked, trying a different angle.

"Again with the safe. I say this with the utmost sincerity. I truly know nothing about the safe you're describing. Don't you think if I'd memorized the safe combination numbers, I would've opened the one in your house holding the evidence that put me away?" he asked.

He had an excellent point, having had total access to the mansion before I inherited it. "But it was hidden behind a painting on the wall," I said, unwilling to swallow his sneaky explanation.

"Who do you think put that picture up before you moved in? I had no idea you were so meddlesome and nosy. Otherwise, I would've installed an entire sheet of drywall to cover it up," he said, reaching out for my hand. Wesley pulled it off the table immediately.

"Sounds like this visit is over since you have no information for us," said Wesley, rising while hitting the buzzer on the wall for the guard to come retrieve us. "Decker, let's go."

Ugh. I needed more time. I leaned over the table and whispered into Grant's ear. "Please help me. I'll figure out a way to get you the cupcakes if you tell me who else knew about the safe lock code," I pleaded. "And I won't tell anyone that you stole the prototype Aston Martin sitting in your sister's garage."

My last statement seized Grant's attention. "You've been harboring a stolen car?"

"You're the one who stole it," I said, knowing full well that Marcus was already working out a deal with the CEO of Aston Martin.

"Finders keepers. Possession is nine-tenths of the law," said Grant. "Sounds like it belongs to you now."

When I didn't move, Wesley came over and tugged my elbow, pulling me all the way out the door.

"What was that about?" he asked.

"I tried to appeal to his more sensitive side and see if he'd whisper some more information to me," I said.

"And did he?" asked Wesley.

Not exactly. I simply groaned in response.

"Decker, forget about him. He's a criminal. And more importantly, a sophisticated con artist who ran insurance scams on stolen cars. He never intended to help us," said Wesley.

I cringed when he said the words *stolen cars*. "Then why did we come up here if you doubted he would give us anything we could use?" I asked.

"So I could babysit you and be sure you wouldn't come up here on your own and get yourself into trouble," said Wesley.

18

Wesley's friend, Joe Bonetti, came out to meet us as we exited the visitor room. This was perfect. Maybe we could all go out for dinner and I could get some fun dirt on Wesley, which would make this whole trip not a total waste.

"Is your boyfriend Marcus Palmer, the tech billionaire genius?" asked Joe.

Ugh. Not again. "No. I mean, he's a friend and he's a boy but he's not my boyfriend," I said.

We hadn't even kissed. Not that kissing someone would assign them the immediate title of boyfriend but it was at least, a step in the right direction. The most we'd ever done was hold hands, solve a murder, and Facetime each other a few times. That definitely did not comprise boyfriend status. "Wait. Why?"

"Apparently, he's here to see you," said Joe, pointing the way to a stairwell that led to the roof. "He must have a lot of connections. He got special clearance to land on our helipad."

All three of us headed up to the roof. Thankfully, it was

only three floors so I wasn't wheezing too badly once we reached the top. It was the same fancy-looking helicopter in the Palmer Tech brand colors of royal blue and gold that picked me up outside Bangor. The door opened and Marcus stepped out, looking just as handsome as he did last night. His flawless, dark ebony skin and chiseled features captured my attention as always. And as usual, he wore khaki shorts, a heather grey tee shirt, and flip-flops.

Marcus and Wesley exchanged nods and he shook Joe's hand before coming over to me.

"What are you doing here?" I screamed as loud as I could to be heard over the helicopter rotors.

Joe interjected, repeating he was here to see me, which I heard the first time but still didn't understand.

"I heard my favorite baker was in trouble so I came right away," said Marcus with his classic, boy-next-door smile.

"Trouble?" I asked. I just saw him last night.

"I saw you on Ten Minutes With Tessa this morning and you were covered in bank dye pack ink and then I saw you at the Clover Creek Police Station and then you were en route to Statesville Penitentiary," he said, pointing to my Palmer Tech SmartWatch he gave me as a present when I first met him. I kept forgetting it had GPS tracking. But even if I remembered, I wouldn't expect the CEO of a multi-billion dollar corporation to take the time to bother checking up on my whereabouts, even if we were friends. "When you didn't answer your phone, I got worried."

I couldn't help feeling a little bit giddy that Marcus would take the trouble to fly here in a helicopter to see me. I smiled as I ran up to hug him. "Thanks. That's really sweet and extremely thoughtful of you but I'm fine. It's just a really long story," I hollered. Too long for me to yell from a prison rooftop.

Marcus and I took off for Clover Creek in his private helicopter while Wesley benevolently agreed to drive back on his own. I knew I should've at least offered to accompany Wesley but after the two-hour drive, followed by the four-hour wait, I was exhausted. A ten-minute helicopter ride sounded much more appealing.

Barely fifteen minutes passed during our trip but it was enough time for me to tell Marcus everything that happened today between the dye pack kitty string debacle to the dead-end prison visit.

"Can you take me back home? I forgot my phone in Wesley's car and Chloe has been cat-sitting Lucky all day for me. She's probably wondering where I am," I said. Chloe had a key to my house as well as Frosted. Well, technically being a locksmith, she had a key to the entire town but she frequently cat-sat for me so I had a spare set made for her.

"I can take you wherever you want to go but you can also check your messages and make calls on the Palmer Tech SmartWatch I gave you," he said, reaching for my wrist. I meant to read the owner's manual. I really did but I tended to procrastinate about those things. Not only was I wearing a non-working Mickey Mouse watch I'd worn my entire life when I met Marcus, I never really noticed it was broken.

He tapped and swiped a few times on the watch face, demonstrating the steps he took before handing it back to me. There were three messages. The first one was from Chloe telling me that she got an emergency locksmith call and had to go out to Glendale, the next town over, but she dropped Lucky off with Shelby.

The second message was from Shelby who confirmed she was watching Lucky at my place and he was having fun with Skye.

The third message was from Ben's mother, Evelyn, telling me that she hired a lawyer and planned to sue me for the engagement ring Ben gave me. Wonderful!

"Wow, I had no idea this entire time the watch could do all that," I said, which wasn't surprising. I barely knew how to use it to tell time. Giving me a watch like this was like asking a toddler to manage a nuclear power plant. I had no idea how it functioned, what it did, or how to interact with it.

"Didn't you hear the beeps every time you got a new text or call?" asked Marcus.

"Oh, yeah, I did but I thought maybe it was just broken," I said. It also woke me up earlier than I wanted to get up on more than one occasion.

"Then why didn't you say something if you thought it was defective?" asked Marcus, clearly confused about my lackadaisical attitude towards technology.

"Well, it was a gift. I didn't want to hurt your feelings by saying that you gave me a faulty watch. I mean, it's the thought that counts, right?" I asked.

"Hmmm, I see," said Marcus, simply nodding his head. It was probably safe to say there were no more Palmer Tech gifts in my future.

19

Our diamond sleuthing club reconvened at my place with one of our standard staples: lobster rolls and cheese fries from the Little Dog Diner and root beer floats. One perk to having a friend with a helicopter is swooping into a neighboring town for your favorite lobster rolls in five minutes flat.

Skye perched herself onto Marcus's shoulder like a parrot.

"What a little flirt. Skye never does that with me," said Shelby, taking a sip of her root beer float.

"Me, neither. Maybe it's a sign you should get an Abyssinian kitten of your own," I said, giving Skye a little neck rub as I leaned over to grab another french fry.

"I travel too often for that but I do love cats. Maybe I could hang out with Lucky more frequently when I'm in town to get my kitty fix," said Marcus, petting Skye.

"But Lucky is always with me," I said, dipping my French fry into the cheese dip.

"I know," said Marcus with a smile.

"Oh," was all I could utter. The heat flamed in my

cheeks and I quickly changed the subject back to our investigation. "So who's left on our diamond thief suspect list?"

I walked over to the whiteboard and crossed off the names of Grant and Chloe, which left only Melanie, which I also crossed out.

"Wesley confirmed Melanie's alibi. She was out of town on Friday when the diamond was stolen," I said before I added Madame Omega to the suspect list. Shelby gave me a confused look.

"The only way she could've known the diamond would be stolen is if she planned it herself," I said.

"She's a psychic. You can't suspect her just for having a magical gift," said Shelby, jumping up to the whiteboard to wipe Madame Omega's name off the board.

"I know you like her but there's no such thing as psychics," I said, writing Madame Omega back on the board.

"Then how do you explain why she knows everything that's going to happen each week? I see her every Sunday and she predicts my entire week, out to a tee for me," she said, wiping Madame Omega's name off again.

"You see her every single week?" I asked, trying to sound inquisitive instead of judgmental. I was about to write her name on the board again but this time, Shelby threw her body in front of it.

"How else am I supposed to plan out my life?" asked Shelby, like it was a silly question.

This was like arguing that Santa Claus wasn't real. I made a mental note to add Madame Omega back on the whiteboard after Shelby went home for the night.

"All right, let's move onto our next diamond suspect," I said, gently nudging Shelby out of the way so I could add Tyler's name to the board.

"All right, now you're just putting random names on the

board for no reason. Why would Tyler steal his own ring?" Shelby promptly wiped his name off the board.

I brought Shelby up to speed on my visit to Grant.

"He didn't mention anything to me about it but I'm sure there's a perfectly logical explanation," said Shelby, still guarding the whiteboard from me.

"Great, then let's ask him," I said. I walked over to her spot on the couch and grabbed her phone and dialed Tyler, putting it on speakerphone.

Shelby tried to hit the red *end* button but I was expecting that and pulled the phone out of her reach before she could do it.

"Don't you want to know why Tyler didn't tell you about visiting Grant? And why he asked him about the lock code for the safe?" I asked, pushing the phone towards Shelby. I didn't want to add Tyler to the suspect pool but seeing his name on the Statesville visitor log and Grant's claim that he was asking about the safe were highly suspicious.

"I'm from the South. I was raised to be polite and to quietly mention my concerns in passing. Direct confrontation is considered both rude and in extremely poor taste," she said.

"Hello, beautiful," said Tyler when he answered the phone. "How's kitty-sitting at Ava's going? Do you need some company?"

Aww, that was cute. Now that was definitely flirting. I pushed the phone towards her. She couldn't hang up now.

"It's going great. Ava actually had a question for you," she said, pushing the phone back to me like it was a hot potato. She gave me the ohmigosh look, which was fine. I was done with the *let's check things out tomorrow* approach.

"Hey, Tyler, I actually have some good news. Marcus found the real owner of that fancy sports car sitting in my garage," I said trying to segue smoothly into my Grant-related questions.

"Wonderful. Do you need me to help you with the paperwork?" asked Tyler.

"No, it's actually stolen, and Grant confirmed that today when I talked to him in person," I said, leaning over the phone to get closer to the mic.

I couldn't be sure but I thought I heard Tyler gasp on the other end. "You spoke to Grant in person? You went to Statesville? That's over two hours away."

He would know since he only recently made the trip himself.

"Yes, and the funny thing is he said I wasn't his only visitor this month. It sounds like you went to visit him, too," I said, feigning uncertainty.

Tyler stammered before mouthing the beginnings of a few incoherent dribbles.

"Tyler?" I asked. "We can't hear you. Are you still there?"

We all held our breaths, waiting for an answer.

"Yes, I'm here. I went to see Grant for the same reason. I purchased all my cars from him and had some car questions," said Tyler.

Good save but I wasn't buying it and neither were Shelby and Marcus, judging by the looks on their faces.

"So you didn't go there to ask him for the safe lock code at Frosted?" I asked.

"What? No! Why would I do that? I didn't even know you owned a safe until last Friday when the diamond was stolen," said Tyler. "And why would I ask Grant about it?"

"Grant said you pretended to be his lawyer to ask him about the safe," I replied. "He bought it for his sister when she owned the bakery. Your firm processed all the paperwork for him."

"Well, he's lying. I never asked him about the safe," said Tyler. "My sister handled everything for him."

"Then why would you need to ask him about your cars?" I asked.

Tyler let out a huge sigh. "Because just like the car in your garage, all of mine are stolen too," he said.

"That's okay. We were both duped by Grant. No one knew he was stealing all of those foreign luxury cars," I said. "Everyone thought his dealership was completely legit."

Tyler let out a groan. "Not everyone. Grant said he was having cash flow problems and he paid for all the legal work I did for him with the stolen cars. He didn't outright say they were stolen but I knew it. It seemed like a harmless crime."

That explained why Tyler could afford so many exotic sports cars. They were all free.

"So why visit him now?" I asked. Not that I condoned stealing cars but it did seem like a harmless crime.

"The FBI has started an inventory reconciliation with Interpol on stolen cars. Grant called me to blackmail me. If I didn't find a way to get him out of prison, he threatened to tell the FBI where to find the missing cars, which is in my garage," he said. "He wanted me to work out some deal with the DA but the cars aren't worth enough to warrant even an initial meeting. I already turned them into the FBI today."

Shelby picked up the phone and took it off speaker. "I knew you were innocent, honey bunny. I told Ava there was a perfectly good explanation for you being at the prison. I never doubted you for a second," she said, taking the phone with her into the other room for privacy.

Lucky followed her into the kitchen. "Lucky thinks you're going to give him kitty treats," I hollered after her.

"I can do that," she answered back.

Skye was not food motivated and preferred to stay glued to Marcus, the new object of her affection.

"Well, at least, we can clear one name off the list," said Marcus, holding Skye in one hand and reaching for a handful of fries with the other.

I went to the whiteboard and put Madame Omega back on the diamond suspect list.

"Shelby's not going to be happy when she sees you've added her again and besides, maybe she really is a psychic. Weirder things have been known to happen," he said.

"First, aren't you a man of science? And second, there's no such thing as psychics," I insisted. Then I huddled closer to Marcus and whispered my new theory. "If I had someone like Shelby coming over every week, she'd be a big cash cow I couldn't risk losing. I'd have to either hire a PI or simply start following her and her boyfriend around to get to know them better if only to make more educated guesses at her readings."

I briefed him on the whole wind swooshing light show she put on with her crystal ball when I visited her.

"All right, let's say Madame Omega finds out about the ring and plans to steal it for herself. Wouldn't telling Shelby ahead of time that it's going to be stolen tip Shelby off to her plan?" he asked, dragging a silver piece of string along the couch for Skye to attack.

"What if she orchestrated the whole thing to set herself up as a consultant to the police for extra cash? The police use psychics all the time to help them solve crimes. This would only further legitimize her," I said.

"I'm not sure you're giving the police enough credit. Wesley seems pretty sharp and not someone who'd fall so easily for a charlatan act like a psychic," said Marcus, switching over to a fuzzy ball and throwing that for Skye to chase across the room.

"Fair enough but just in case, let's bolster our accusation with some evidence, like the actual diamond," I said.

"Don't you think she pawned it already?" asked Marcus.

"I bet she hid it and is waiting for the perfect moment to have a vision, then she tips off the police and comes out as the hero psychic who solves crimes," I said, using air quotes for the word *vision*. "We need to find that diamond. It has to be hidden somewhere at her store."

"Or it could be inside a safety deposit box, with a friend for safekeeping, under the floorboards in her apartment," said Marcus, pulling up his SmartWatch and typing a few things in.

"What are you doing?" I asked after writing down all those ideas on the whiteboard.

"Checking to see if she has a Palmer Tech SmartWatch," he said. "Which, unfortunately, she does not."

"Yet," I said. "Tomorrow. You go there for a reading and pay her with a SmartWatch and then we can track her. If I stole a one hundred thousand-dollar ring, I'd want to check on it from time to time," I said.

Marcus gave me a thumbs-up as he inhaled another lobster roll.

After Marcus and Shelby left, I called Caitlin to confirm she could open the bakery by herself in the morning so I could sleep in. It was silly but there was something about sitting around for long hours at a time that exhausted me. I even turned off the front gate intercom box. There was nothing in this world that could convince me to get up before noon tomorrow.

Nothing, that is, except the police tearing down my door and arresting me for grand theft auto.

20

It was a shame that after I finally learned how to use my Palmer Tech Smartwatch to call out, it was one of the first things the police confiscated when they arrested me. Wesley promised to call Chloe to come over and watch Lucky and then Marcus, to see if he reached out to his Aston Martin contact.

"Nice pajamas," said Grandpa Lockwood as I entered the police station. I was wearing my Cookie Monster cotton pajamas from high school. What could I say? They were comfy and I wasn't expecting company.

"Thanks. They didn't let me get dressed," I called out as I passed by the front desk. They literally dragged me from my bed and marched me out in handcuffs, as if I were a super dangerous criminal that could evade capture at any minute. If I'd possessed that particular skill, I might not have been in the predicament I was in now.

"Don't worry, Ava. I know you didn't steal that car," he called out as I made my way closer to the reception desk he manned. "We'll get this sorted out right away."

"Thanks and if I'd known I would be arrested today for

grand theft auto, I would've baked some cupcakes to bring along for you this morning," I said.

He patted me gently on the back as I sat down for processing. "If I could let you go, I would, but they assigned some bigwig federal agents on the case since the car is worth over a million dollars," said Grandpa Lockwood.

A million dollars? FBI? It all sounded really scary. Being on good terms with the Lockwoods couldn't help me now if the Feds were in charge of my arrest. My only hope was that Marcus would come through. Of all the things that I thought I might end up in jail for doing, the last thing on my list would have been a stolen car. Guess it was my punishment for procrastinating and not dealing with it earlier. This was actually my best friend, Ruby's fault. I told her I wanted to know all about the car as soon as Grant was arrested but she told me to forget it and leave well enough alone.

"Why didn't the FBI come for the car sooner?" I asked. That car was sitting in my garage undisturbed and unbeknownst to anyone except Tyler, Marcus and Shelby until two days ago. Now the entire world knew about it. Maybe it was a tech activation thing. When Marcus started the engine for the first time, it probably sent an overseas signal to the Aston Martin headquarters in the U.K., alerting them to the car's exact location.

"That shady shyster, Grant, worked out a deal with the District Attorney to reduce his sentence in exchange for information on the whereabouts of a stolen three million-dollar car," replied Grandpa Lockwood.

Ugh. Grant. Of course. I could kick myself for even bothering to ask him about it. Of course, it was stolen and of course, Grant knew exactly where it was and how to use that information to his advantage. Up until my visit yesterday, Grant probably assumed the car had been seized in the initial dissolution of his luxury car dealership. According to Tyler, it wasn't even on the missing inventory list from his dealership. Leave it to me to provide him with just the right information to put me away. Wesley was right. Grant was nothing more than a con artist and he completely scammed me yesterday.

The nice thing about being arrested previously, (multiple times in fact!) was: you were already in the system. The paperwork and processing time were cut in half and my prior fear was significantly reduced because it felt more like a reunion visit rather than a scary new experience.

"Any update on Dale the Dairy Farmer's murder?" I asked in almost a whisper to Grandpa Lockwood.

"Ahh, did you get arrested on purpose so you could solve another murder case before the police did?" he asked with a wink. I was about to protest my innocence, saying I wasn't that devious nor would that have ever occurred to me but Grandpa Lockwood kept talking. "They did find tire tracks of a delivery truck and it was not Dale's."

Uh-oh. Frosted owned a delivery truck. "Do they know who the vehicle might belong to?" I asked.

"Don't worry. Your cupcake truck tires were the first ones they checked and you've already been cleared," he said.

Of course, they did. When could I escape being the prime suspect in any murders in this town? "How many delivery trucks are there in the Blueberry Bay area?" Clover Creek was a small town but growing, as were the surrounding areas. At the Blueberry Country Fair in April, there were at least thirty food truck vendors for that one event, alone.

"According to the DMV, there are only fifteen currently registered in Clover Creek but the delivery truck could've been from anywhere. They're going through Dale's financials now to search for any invoices for companies with delivery trucks," he said.

"Can I make a phone call?" I asked Grandpa Lockwood when he finished. You always got to make a phone call on TV and in the movies. I never had to ask for that privilege before since people were always with me when I was arrested previously.

"Sure," he said, lifting the receiver on the phone at the front desk and holding it out for me.

I looked at the phone and then at Grandpa Lockwood. I had no one's number memorized. That's what cell phones were for.

"Any chance I could use my cell phone or my SmartWatch?" I asked, nodding towards the basket that contained all of my belongings locked up in a Ziploc bag and labeled *evidence*. He did a small eye roll and gave me a speech about the dangers of relying too heavily on technology but handed me my phone.

I called Ruby. No answer. That left Shelby or Marcus. I wasn't sure who was a better bet and before I had a chance to decide, the phone rang. It was Marcus.

"Don't worry, Ava. The head of Aston Martin is on the line right now with the FBI. He can clear this all up for you," he said.

"Thanks, but how did you know?" I asked.

"The SmartWatch tells me your GPS even when you take it off. Your heart rate was off the charts this morning. At first, I thought you might have been going out for a run but the velocity at which you were traveling clearly indicated you were in a car; and then, of course, your destination told me everything else I needed to know," he said.

"But how did you know to call the FBI?" I asked. I

assumed he would have called the police to get me released, not the FBI.

"Who do you think supplies the watches for their field agents?" he asked, like that explained everything and protected him carte blanche, even if his friends broke the law. "I called in a favor to see what was going on."

He could do that? So this was what it felt like to have friends in high places with connections.

"But they've already arrested me and are preparing to put me into a holding cell," I said, feeling hopeful but not wanting to get too excited.

"Trust me, you'll be out by the time I hang up this phone. I'm on my way there now to pick you up," he said.

True to his word, the FBI agents that previously swarmed my house not only let me know that I was free to go, but they also apologized for wrongly arresting me and asked for my forgiveness.

"Our apologies, ma'am. We were told on good authority that you were a lethally dangerous criminal, which was why we wore body armor and had our assault weapons trained on you," said the lead FBI agent who brought me in.

When I didn't say anything due to sheer shock and uncertainty over whether or not I was hallucinating, Grandpa Lockwood elbowed me in the side and pushed me forward.

"As long as you promise never to call me *ma'am* again, all is forgiven. Besides, I go to the police station all the time so you basically did me a favor by giving me a ride and helping me to get a head start on the day," I said.

Wesley came out just then and put his head in his hands, clearly disappointed by my speech to the FBI agents. "The only thing she's a danger to is your waistline with her stuffed cupcake bakery," he said, sipping down the rest of his spirulina smoothie.

"Of course, ma'am. I'm sorry. I mean, miss," said the FBI agent.

"Free cupcakes for everyone today at Frosted," I said, pointing toward the bakery, which was only a short walk away.

Grandpa Lockwood offered to take them there and get them situated while I texted Caitlin to let her know to expect them. I was so glad I arranged for her to open the bakery this morning for me.

I grabbed my belongings from the evidence bag and headed toward the front doors. It was a nice, warm summer day, or at least it was from what I remembered on the drive over. While the entire ordeal was pretty painless, despite having to endure the scare of my life in waking up to a bedroom full of men with machine guns pointed at me, I was more than ready to get out of the police station and embrace my freedom.

"Hey wait," Wesley called out, trotting out after me. "Here are your keys. I just need you to sign this release form and the car is all yours."

"But it was stolen. Why are you giving it back to me?" I asked. "Oh, wait. Am I responsible for returning this car to the factory in London?" The cost of that would be beyond belief expensive but it sure beat having to sit in jail for ten years, the maximum sentence for grand theft auto in Massachusetts.

"You mean back to Aston Martin's headquarters in England?" he asked.

"Yes, that's who owns the car," I said.

"The CEO of Aston Martin just told the FBI that the car belongs to you and there was simply a technical glitch in their system during the filing of the sales paperwork," he said.

All right, it was official. I was still pleasantly asleep in my bed and must have been dreaming. Or inside a jail cell already and dreaming on my cot.

"All right, great," I said, swiping the keys from his hand and signing the papers on his clipboard. I was finally having a dream that benefited me. Instead of questioning it, I decided to just go with it.

He ripped off the carbon copy underneath. "Did you want a copy?" he asked, trying to catch up with me on my sprint to the doors and out of the police station.

"Nope, I'm good," I said, quickening my pace towards the last few steps to the outside.

"Don't you even want to know where the car is parked?" asked Wesley.

21

My happy dream was instantly transformed into a nightmare when I flung open the police doors and descended the steps at full speed, running straight into a huge Channel Five news camera focused on me. But that wasn't the worst part. I was used to seeing Tessa at my worst moments but this time, she had my ex-fiance's mother beside her. While I sometimes did miss my ex-fiance, Ben, I never once missed his overbearing mother, Evelyn.

It looked like the millions Ben won in the lottery the morning of our wedding were spent on Prada and Birken bags, along with copious amounts of tacky perfume. Not only was Evelyn covered in designer clothes and accessories but also dripping in diamonds. She shot me a hateful glare before turning back to the cameras to smile.

"You're live with Ten Minutes With Tessa. We're here to meet Ava Decker, the diamond engagement ring thief. No surprise that this isn't the first diamond engagement ring she's stolen. Isn't that right, Mrs. Yardley?" asked

Tessa, placing the microphone in front of Evelyn's smug face.

"Yes, that's exactly what happened. Ava Decker pretended to care for my sweet, darling Ben just to steal the beautiful diamond engagement ring that he spent a fortune on," said Evelyn Yardley, pretending to dab away some fake tears.

A fortune? As if! After checking with five different pawn shops, I could only recover three hundred dollars for it. Not nearly worth the ten years of my life it cost me.

"The money from that ring barely even put a dent in all the ridiculously expensive, over-the-top wedding extras you insisted I purchase for you, never mind the entire cost of the wedding and the honeymoon I never had," I said, crossing my arms in defiance.

Her days of bullying me were so over. I let her convince me to buy crazy expensive rare and exotic flowers and table settings for the wedding, along with a private limousine to chauffeur her and her friends all over town "prepping" for the wedding, as well as her dress and accessories for the day. She insisted her dress be equal in cost to mine.

"Everyone knows the bride is supposed to pay for the wedding. Your days of diamond stealing are over. If it's the last thing I do, I will make you pay, Ava Decker. I bent over backwards to get you a special discount on your waterfront wedding reception at my private yacht club," said Evelyn with a scoff.

"Are you referring to the five thousand-dollar catering fee you got a kickback on and kept for yourself?" I asked. Technically, it was supposed to be a discount in the form of a member referral reimbursement but Evelyn pocketed the money instead of passing it on to me.

Before Evelyn had a chance to answer, Tessa interrupted. "And you believe that Ava stole the diamond ring you saw in the news because of her history of stealing diamond engagement rings?" asked Tessa.

"Of course! Wasn't that why the police arrested her this morning?" she asked with a haughty glance my way.

"No. I got arrested for grand theft auto!" I blurted out before I could stop myself, getting so mad at all her false accusations and how she always twisted the truth. "A crime I was instantly cleared of because I didn't steal anything, including anyone's diamond engagement ring," I quickly added.

"That's exactly what a gold-digging con artist would say," said Evelyn, squinting her eyes at me. "After I'm through with you, you'll never be able to show your face again anywhere."

I opened my mouth to argue with her, since she was clearly wrong, until I spotted Marcus in the background. He was driving up and I remembered that I didn't care what anyone thought anymore, especially not this hateful woman who'd done nothing but insulted me and tried to make my life miserable every chance she got.

Not only was my life a thousand times better without Ben and his evil mother, but I was also way happier than I'd ever been during the entire ten years Ben and I dated. I liked looking forward, not behind.

"What car did you steal?" asked Tessa, refocusing her attention and her mic back on me.

"She stole nothing because she owns the car," said Marcus, hopping up the steps and slinging a supportive arm around me.

"Well, that conniving hussy definitely didn't own the diamond ring she stole from my son," said Evelyn, pointing an accusatory finger in my face. "I will not let you get away with this. You're going to regret the day you ever met me."

Like, I didn't already?

"You're Tyler's mom?" asked Marcus.

22

My limited experience dodging Tessa was nothing compared to the Houdini act Marcus pulled off. He lit up a smoke bomb he took out of his pocket and guided me into his car, which was waiting at the curb.

"I'd like to admit I was impressed but that wouldn't even begin to describe how in awe of you I am right now," I said, giving him a hug once we were safely en route from the police station.

"You can thank my sister, Lila, for that one," he said, holding up another smoke bomb. "These were part of her media blitz to add more glamour and excitement to her new beauty gadgets. I had a bunch in my pocket left over from the launch."

Lila was Marcus's little sister who competed in the very first Miss Clover Creek Beauty Pageant that Marcus sponsored in April. While Marcus was a genius at inventing tech accessories to wear, Lila was brilliant too, inventing makeup application gadgets to properly apply eyeliner, shadow, base, and blush. She just introduced her new line last week.

"Yes, please tell her congratulations from me. And thanks again for saving me from grand theft auto charges and a media attack," I said with a smile.

"So that woman wasn't Tyler's mother, but your ex-fiance's mother?" he asked, peeking over his shoulder at the smoke-filled scene still unfolding on the police station steps.

"Unfortunately, yes. And it's true. I hocked the engagement ring instead of returning it, like I should have," I confessed right away. I definitely saw it as mine to keep after he ghosted me at the altar. Being a man, however, Marcus might not see it the same way.

"If you hocked it, then I'm sure you had a very good reason for doing it," he said, patting my hand. "Now, let's see about getting you a proper breakfast, shall we? I'm thinking pancakes, waffles, omelets, the whole works!"

Ahh, that's why I liked Marcus so much. He swiftly avoided awkward confrontations like Tessa, never pried into personal situations that made me uncomfortable, and most importantly, shared my love of food!

Two hours later and still dressed in my pajamas, I had thoroughly enjoyed the world's most extravagant brunch spread I'd ever seen. The Highland Yacht Club (members only!) Brunch Buffet had everything and then some. Not only did it include every breakfast item I could ever want like bacon, eggs, potatoes, and French toast, it also had a raw seafood spread, sushi bar, donuts, bagels, frittatas, omelet stations, noodle bar, pasta bar, and even an ice cream bar.

"They do this every day?" I asked. Maybe I should consider joining the Highland Yacht Club if only to get access to that spread every day.

"Kind of, but not really, no," said Marcus, looking a little flustered.

"Did you do all of that for me?" I asked, slowly rolling myself out the front doors.

"Yes, and I did it especially for you. Just like I bought the roses for you," he said, opening his car door for me. "I'm sorry I made it sound like the roses were a replacement gift or my effort to right a social faux pas. I like making you happy, whether it's with roses or bunch buffets."

"Oh, well, thank you. That's very sweet of you to say, and mission accomplished! I'm extremely happy from both the flowers and the brunch," I said, hopping into Marcus's car. I hoped he couldn't see how red my cheeks were. I felt all squishy inside but it was a good squishy.

Marcus called Wesley before we took off to check on the status of the car that I left behind. According to Wesley, the coast was clear. Tessa, Ben's mother, and the FBI finally all left.

"I hope you know that you can obviously have that super fancy sports car. I know you paid for it and I very much appreciate the kindness, but I don't know how to drive a manual transmission and it's way too luxurious for me," I said. Plus, I was afraid I'd break it.

"You don't think you deserve nice, luxurious things?" asked Wesley, backing the car out.

"I didn't say that," I answered. Or did I? I was simply stating that my style was more utilitarian when it came to cars. He needed plenty of space for Lucky to roam around in, like my parents' SUV.

"So you don't think you're smart enough to learn how to drive a stick shift?" he asked, pulling out into traffic.

"I didn't say that, either," I replied. Or did I? I never commented on my intelligence or aptitude for learning a new driving skill but I did shut it down immediately with a big, negative, *I can't* statement.

"Is it because you just don't want a present from me?"

he asked, adjusting the air conditioning settings on the dash.

I let him pay for our lavish, over-the-top yet delightfully enjoyable brunch mostly because I didn't have my purse with me when I was arrested. The staff at the club said they'd put it on his monthly tab. But still. I graciously thanked him for brunch and only half-heartedly offered to reimburse him. That counted as accepting a present, right?

"The car was a present?" I asked. "From you to me?"

"Sure, why not?" he said.

"Not that I don't appreciate everything you've done for me, but saving me from a ten-year grand theft auto sentence is pretty much already well above and beyond the call of duty," I explained. Not that I didn't love getting gifts just as much as the next person but a three million-dollar car seemed a little steep, even when the friend in question was a billionaire like Marcus Palmer.

"Well, you are my favorite baker," he said with a wink.

Jeez. What did he buy his favorite maid? A chateau in the French Alps? "Well, you've definitely earned Frosted VIP status." Not that there was such a thing, but offering him free cupcakes for life seemed like the least I could do in return.

23

Two painful hours of grinding the gears and popping the clutch later, Marcus and I finally made it back to my house. We were in my now legitimately owned, specially ordered, three million-dollar Aston Martin Valkyrie. Marcus was so excited about teaching me to drive a manual transmission, that his entire face lit up when I finally agreed to learn.

"Don't worry, tomorrow will be much better," said Marcus, giving me a pat on the back.

"Tomorrow?" I repeated. Is that how learning to drive a stick shift worked? After a good night's sleep, I magically knew how to drive it the next day?

"Yes, we'll practice together every day until you catch on," he said. Oh, no! There was no magic involved. Just hard work and persistence.

"Great, I'll be ready to compete in the Formula One series by this time next week," I said with as much zeal as I could muster. I was sincerely trying to learn, but the art of listening to the engine and feeling for when to shift gears was definitely not happening. I was a very methodical, exact measurement type of gal. I needed clear, concrete directions, telling me exactly what to do and when, precisely, like my recipes or even my former accounting job. If the car would simply ring a bell or something told me what gear to shift into, I'd happily comply.

The seating in the Valkyrie was as narrow as my cupcake truck was wide. Because it was built as a Formula One racing car, the two-passenger compartment was basically a tiny bubble in the middle while the rest of the car fanned out wide on the front and back, kind of like a spider. Marcus was practically glued to my right side. Each time Marcus guided my hand to the correct gear, I flushed red, and my cheeks were burning at his touch. I nearly crashed the car into the garage by the time we finished. I was completely distracted by the butterflies in my core.

"Which crime should we revisit investigating first? The missing diamond ring or the dairy farmer murder?" asked Marcus, rubbing his hands together in anticipation as we entered the house. "While you were busy being arrested, I gave a SmartWatch to Madame Omega and have been tracking her movements. So far nothing. She bought a pretzel from the stand outside but otherwise has been at her shop all morning."

I again remembered why I liked Marcus so much. He was always part of the solution and he never tried to impede or hinder my investigative pursuits.

"Great work. Do I even want to ask what your fortune was?" I replied as we entered the main room and our whiteboard of suspects.

"She predicted lots of cupcakes in my future," he said, taking a seat on the couch.

Did he mean that in a romantic way? Or just as a dessert aficionado?

"You have cupcakes? I didn't see any in the fridge," said Chloe, coming out from the kitchen with Lucky.

Lucky bounced over and jumped up into my arms, licking my face. "Aww, I missed you, too, little guy. Thanks so much for watching him. I can easily whip up a batch of cupcakes as soon as I wash some of this prison grime off me." Along with some *Nutella* and chocolate syrup that fell on my shirt from breakfast.

"It's okay. I need to head back to work so I'll take a rain check on those cupcakes," said Chloe, grabbing her keys off the front door hook before she ran out.

While Marcus played with Lucky out in the living room, I headed upstairs and took a quick shower and put on some regular clothes. Being the gentleman he was, Marcus didn't once comment on or question my Cookie Monster pajamas.

Once I emerged, we migrated to the kitchen where I quickly whipped up a batch of cupcakes and threw them in the oven. I poured some lactose-free milk for Lucky and then made Mexican Mocha Lattes for Marcus and me. I offered him some of the new filled cupcakes creations I was experimenting with and he gladly accepted, diving right in without even asking what flavors they were.

"You make the very best filled cupcakes in the world. And I would know, having visited over two hundred countries and I can confirm no pastry chef even comes close," said Marcus, already reaching for his second cupcake.

"Thanks, these are new flavors I'm trying out. You just had the Pumpkin Spiced Caramel Cupcakes with Cream Cheese Filling, which I'm testing out for October. And now you're eating the French Vanilla Cheesecake Filled Cupcakes, which I created to go with the Mexican Mocha Lattes," I said, taking a sip from my mug.

"Sign me up. I'm totally in," said Marcus, taking

another bite. While he finished eating, I cleaned up the kitchen and put everything away.

Marcus's SmartWatch beeped like crazy. He looked down at it and announced, "It looks like Madame Omega is on the move... going to get groceries at the local Stop-N-Shop."

"Not likely she hid the diamond there," I said. So much for my genius idea on Madame Omega surveillance.

"It's still early. I'll keep watching for anything out of the ordinary," said Marcus.

Lucky stomped on his now empty kitty bowl and groaned, signaling that he wanted more.

"Hey, little guy. That was a lot of milk. What about switching to some kitty kibble?" I asked, pouring a few into his food bowl. He sniffed it and gave me an accusatory look, like I just offered him broccoli and lima beans. When I didn't respond, he stuck his paw in the bowl and flicked the kibbles out, sending them soaring into the air. "Lucky, that was not very nice."

Marcus dropped to his knees and helped me pick them up and place them back in Lucky's bowl.

"I guess he knows what he wants and the little dude likes milk," said Marcus. "I can get him some more, if that's okay." He went to the fridge and retrieved the lactose-free milk bottle. Lucky recognized the bottle on sight and started jumping up and down, dancing little kitty circles around his bowl. A series of excited meows of happiness spewed out of his kitty mouth. Who could say no to that cute, little, kitty milk dance?

"Sure but just a little bit," I replied. Before Marcus could even finish pouring, Lucky's face was already diving in the bowl and lapping it up. With Lucky occupied, we went back to studying the whiteboard out in the main room.

"The problem this time is a total and complete lack of

potential suspects," said Marcus. "There's no one for us to hunt down and look deeper into."

He was right. Normally, it was a matter of chasing down all the leads and separating the lies from the half-truths but this time, we had nothing.

After hitting a dead end on our whiteboard suspect-gathering exercise, Marcus and I called it a night, which was fine by me. I was so exhausted, I didn't even notice the kitty neck sweater smothering me all night.

Wednesday morning had to be infinitely better than today. There was nowhere to go but up from here.

24

I was right. Wednesday was already off to a stellar start.

First, I woke up in my bedroom alone, sans the FBI and police department. Second, I had zero concerns about secretly harboring a stolen car in my garage. And third, I made it to Frosted in time to help Caitlin bake today's cupcakes.

This was going to be a great day.

A bike messenger pulled up to the back door of Frosted and knocked before poking his head inside. For a brief second, I worried that it was Wesley coming to chastise me for leaving the back door open again.

"Ava Decker?" he asked, walking up to me.

"Yes, that's me," I said.

"You've been served," he said, shoving a brown manila envelope at me.

I opened it up. True to her word, Ben's mother was suing me for the ring. Not only the original five hundred dollars that Ben paid for it but also millions of dollars in emotional distress she claimed that I inflicted upon her, the wedding guests, and her precious Ben.

And just like that, my wonderful morning turned to mush. I barely had enough money to keep Frosted open and still make my credit card payments, much less, pay for a lawyer. No way did I have millions to pay for her lawsuit and even if I did, I'd rather die than let a single penny go to her.

"What was that?" asked Caitlin, pulling her AirPods out.

"The mailman," I said, folding up the lawsuit and pocketing it in my apron.

"Coming to the backdoor?" she asked, crinkling her forehead.

"It's all that construction outside for the underground trolley they're building. I think the alleyway was faster," I said.

She accepted that as a logical answer, put her AirPods back in, and resumed dancing around while she baked. I let her know I was heading out but I'd be back later.

I picked up a box of French Vanilla Cheesecake Filled Cupcakes and a Mexican Mocha Latte for Grandpa Lockwood before heading out to the Clover Creek police station, only this time, it was voluntary.

When you weren't being hauled in against your will, the old-style, white bulb gas lamps flanking the cement steps leading up to the double doors out front were actually very picturesque. I never really appreciated the dated architecture and historic features of Clover Creek when I was growing up, but now that I had returned after being away for ten years, I felt proud of my small town.

"You must really want some information pretty bad if you're bringing me a fancy, foamy drink to go with my cupcakes," said Grandpa Lockwood, taking a big gulp of the Mexican Mocha Latte before I could warn him of the spice factor. "Whoa, Nelly!" He pounded the police reception counter with his fist a few times. "Now, that'll wake you up in the morning."

"It has a little kick to it," I said, pointing to the latte. The cayenne pepper was not only fresh but minced right before serving to ensure it kept the original oils that gave it that extra oomph.

"Hold on," said Grandpa Lockwood as he jumped up and ran over to the water fountain. "All right, now what can I help you with this morning?"

"I wanted to thank you for chaperoning all the Federal agents down to Frosted yesterday," I said, trying to ease into the conversation.

"Free stuffed cupcakes and lattes at my favorite bakery? I'm pretty sure I should be thanking you," he said. "Now, I know why you're really here."

I gave him my most innocent look. "To commend a Clover Creek peace officer for doing such an outstanding job of going above and beyond."

Grandpa Lockwood took a huge bite out of one of the cupcakes. "There must be some truth serum in these cupcakes because I do feel compelled to tell you that the police have classified the missing diamond as a cold case and are no longer investigating it. All of Dale the Dairy Farmer's employees have alibis for the time of his murder except one missing employee. The police are trying to track him down now for questioning. There's a warrant out for his arrest."

He pointed to a Wanted Sign behind the desk. The man's name was Juan Garcia.

"Do you know anything else about him?" I asked, Googling him on my phone. Juan Garcia was a pretty common name and returned a gazillion hits in Clover Creek, alone.

"Nope. That's pretty much all we got. Dale liked to help out the underdog, which included people who are here illegally without work visas. He usually paid everyone in cash so there are no official employee records of any kind," said Grandpa Lockwood. "Now, you didn't hear any of that from me."

"Didn't hear any of what?" asked Wesley, who appeared out of nowhere.

Grandpa Lockwood and I both shrugged our shoulders and played dumb. Wesley simply shook his head, pinching the bridge of his nose as he said, "Why me?"

25

Shelby had the rest of the day off and offered to watch Lucky for me so he and Skye could have an extended kitty playdate.

She lived at the Highland Yacht Club Tower Apartments, right next to the place where Marcus took me to brunch yesterday. She pulled me inside before I could even knock on the door.

"Finally. What took you so long? I need help," she said, in a frenzied voice, pulling me to the windows.

Shelby lived on the penthouse level and her apartment overlooked the front of the building. I unclipped Lucky and asked her, "What are we looking at?"

"Tyler. He's coming here any minute to propose all over again," she said, biting her fingernail.

"That's good news, right?" I asked, feeling confused. Now that Tyler had come clean about the stolen cars and his visit to Grant, there was no reason for Shelby to be worried.

"I've been trying all morning and cannot reach Madame Omega. I can't make this big of a decision without consulting her first," she said before starting to hyperventilate.

I walked her over to the couch, sat her down and told her to prop her feet up on the table. I took a few deep, calming breaths with her and when she finally seemed to relax, I counted backward from ten.

"Feel better?" I asked.

"Yes, a little," she said.

"All right, I'm going to help you figure this out," I said.

"Yes, please," she said with a grateful smile.

"Do you love Tyler?" I asked, to which she nodded.

"And do you trust him and feel like he loves you back?" I asked and she also nodded.

"Does he make you happy?" I asked and she nodded again.

"Do you feel like he's a good person?" I asked and she nodded.

"Is he the one or do you still have doubts or want to see what else is out there?" I asked.

"No, he's for sure the one. He's always so kind to me and all of my friends. He apologized profusely about keeping the car thing from me and I'm totally in love with him," she said with a smile.

"Then what's the problem?" I asked. "You obviously want to marry him."

I handed her a fluffy throw pillow to hold on to. Those always calmed my nerves.

"That's not it. I would just feel better if Madame Omega confirmed my decision. She always knows what I should do," said Shelby, picking up her phone. She dialed Madame Omega's number but it went straight to voicemail.

"You don't need a psychic to tell you what to say. You already know," I said, taking her phone from her and placing it on the table. It took all my willpower to stay focused on calming Shelby down instead of texting Marcus for a GPS update on Madame Omega's whereabouts.

"So it won't hurt to have Madame Omega confirm it first," she said, reaching for her phone again but I blocked her.

"I know it's scary to be an adult and make decisions on your own. I hate making mistakes, too, but sometimes, those are the best parts of life. If I hadn't wasted ten years with the biggest mistake of a fiancé ever, then I would've never come back home to Clover Creek, or inherited my dream bakery and mansion or found Lucky or met you.

"So yes, I could've spent my first ten years out of high school making better choices but then I would've missed out on so much in life by not screwing it up. Life is for living and learning as you go, not doing things perfectly. Plus, that's boring and you, Shelby Hicks, are anything but boring," I said, taking both of her hands in mine. "Now, what's the real reason you're talking to this psychic so much? A possible life crutch? A convenient scapegoat for wany future mistakes?"

Shelby let out a huge sigh. "I guess you're right. I've been using Madame Omega as a crutch. That way, if something goes wrong, I can blame it on her."

"It's easier to make decisions when you have someone else to share in the blame in case things go south," I said. Kind of how I blamed Ruby for my car theft arrest when really I should've listened to my own gut and investigated the mystery car in my garage sooner.

"So what do I say when Tyler comes here?" she asked.

"Whatever's inside your heart," I replied. "If it makes you feel any better, I'm fairly certain that all of my mistakes and bad decisions will pale in comparison to yours. In fact, the mother of one of them just served me with a million-dollar lawsuit this morning."

"What? Oh, no! Do you need Tyler to help you?" she asked.

I pulled the papers out of my pocket. "Actually, yes, if you could pass this along to him and see if it is something he could help me with, that would be great." I had no idea how I could pay him for it but that was a problem for tomorrow.

"Of course, on one condition," she said, taking the papers from me.

"Yes?" I asked.

"You should take your own advice and let yourself make a mistake with Marcus," she said. "He really likes you."

"I thought we were talking about you. And anyway, how do you know he even likes me?" I asked.

Shelby threw the pillow I'd given her back at me. "Oh, right! A man who buys you a three million-dollar car doesn't like you, at all."

"All right, so maybe he likes me a little bit," I said, smiling while thinking about him.

The doorbell rang. We looked over and saw Tyler in the viewfinder. "That's my cue to leave," I said, standing up and giving her a quick hug before dashing out. "Good luck and remember you don't have to make a decision today. If Tyler really loves you, which obviously does, he'll wait until you're ready."

26

I met Marcus back at my place. He confirmed that Madame Omega was on the move. She'd boarded a plane at Bangor airport a few minutes ago which explained why her phone was going straight to voicemail. Since neither of us knew her real name, it was impossible to look up her flight itinerary. We'd just have to wait until she landed to find out her final destination.

"Ready for your next driving lesson?" asked Marcus.

He headed towards my garage but stopped when he noticed that I was still standing outside.

"I promise I'll let you know the minute Madame Omega lands somewhere," he said.

"It's not that," I said and then proceeded to bring him up to speed on what Grandpa Lockwood told me about Dale's murder investigation.

"This Juan Garcia guy, if that's even his real name, is in the wind, according to Grandpa Lockwood. They can't figure out who he is or anything about him," I said.

"On it," said Marcus, punching some commands into his SmartWatch when we slid into my new, overpriced sports car. "All right I have five people with that name in the area but none of them works at Dale's Dairy Farm except one."

"How do you know that?" I asked, closing my door and buckling the seatbelt. With the doors closed, Marcus's sandalwood cologne filled up the car and gave me all tingly feelings inside.

'We're in luck. He has a Palmer Tech SmartWatch. We can track him in real time," said Marcus.

Was this my lucky day or what? We had a new lead in Dale's murder and the suspect was wearing a GPS-enabled tracker.

"Where is he?" I asked. Marcus leaned over the center console so we could both see his watch. Being squished together in a Formula One racing car because there was nowhere else to spread out wasn't the same as standing right next to me. I could feel the bulge of his arm as he leaned towards me. Half of me felt guilty for not going to the gym more often, or ever, and the other half just wanted to be closer to Marcus. "Route Seven, mile marker forty-nine."

"What?" I asked, still in my potential romance reverie.

"Juan Garcia is traveling on Route Seven right now and he just passed mile marker forty-nine," said Marcus, pointing at his watch.

Oh, right. We're tracking a killer down. "That's where Dale's dairy farm is."

"Why would he go back?" asked Marcus.

"To get rid of the evidence? He left in a hurry when the police found Dale's body. Maybe Juan had something important stashed there, like his real identity or the diamond engagement ring," I said. A dairy farm out in the country that paid its employees in cash was the perfect hiding spot for stolen goods or personal belongings you didn't want found.

"I'll call Wesley and let him know," I said, already dialing his cell number. After relaying what Marcus and I discovered, you'd think Wesley would have been out the door and chasing him down but instead, he chose that moment to give me a lecture on minding my own business and staying out of trouble.

"Aren't you worried that Juan Garcia will get away?" I asked.

"I'm more worried that you're going to get yourself killed," he said.

"Have I ever been killed even once?" I asked.

"Seriously, Decker? If this Juan Garcia person really is the killer, you're putting yourself in great danger by going to the dairy farm," said Wesley. "Are you already en route and driving as we speak?"

"What makes you think I'd try to apprehend him? I called you first, didn't I?" I asked.

"Are you already there?" asked Wesley.

"No, don't be silly," I said. After that, Wesley turned on the police sirens and hung up.

"He'll never make it there faster than we can," said Marcus, pointing to the Aston Martin Valkyrie dashboard. He programmed the fastest route to the dairy farm into the GPS. "Come on. Aren't you dying to use seventh gear on this thing?"

"I haven't even gone past fourth gear yet," I replied. The speed limits within the town of Clover Creek were usually twenty and occasionally reached forty-five on the country roads. According to Google, most manual transmissions only came with five gears. If this had seven, I was afraid to even find out what speeding limits I'd have to break in order to need seventh gear.

"Exactly," said Marcus, rubbing his hands together in a

mock sinister pose. "Come on, Ava. Do you want to catch this Juan Garcia character or not?"

Now, that did motivate me. I could solve both the diamond heist and the murder all in one fell swoop. I hopped into the driver's side, pushed the key into the center console like a CD and we took off.

Driving at seventy miles per hour in an SUV high up off the ground felt very different from a Formula One racing car that was mere millimeters off the ground. It was like watching a movie in fast forward.

I made a silent plea to the universe that no Bambis were crossing the road while I made my turn onto Route Seven. The mile markers whizzed by in a blur. I only slowed down when I saw the cow pasture. We made it to the dairy farm in record time. Wesley wasn't even there yet. This time, I drove all the way to the barn at the top instead of stopping at the bottom of the hill.

It was a steep hill with a large crest at the top. By the time we reached the barn, we saw a mystery pick-up truck and two Escalades parked at the top of the hill.

"This doesn't look right," I said to Marcus as we pulled up closer.

Men in windbreakers with the words *U.S. Marshals Service* hopped out of the vehicles and pointed their guns at us.

"Freeze," yelled the one in front. "Step out of your vehicle slowly with your hands raised."

"Any chance this fancy car is bulletproof?" I asked Marcus as I turned the engine off and lifted my hands in the air. I'd never seen a U.S. Marshal before so I was still trying to decide if they were real or fake.

"Not that I know of. It's a Formula One racing car so at best, the special fireproof material might protect us in case the marshals decide to attack us with blowtorches," he said with his hands up in the air.

"Why would the U.S. Marshals be investigating the murder of a dairy farmer?" I asked the man who was now locking me up in handcuffs.

"Why is a pastry chef driving a Formula One race car to a dairy farm?" he asked, hauling me over to the first black Escalade. I was about to ask him how he knew I was a baker until I remembered I was wearing my Frosted employee tee shirt today. It was comfortable, made of cotton and best of all, clean. I was a little remiss on the dirty laundry pile at home.

Wesley chose that moment to finally drive up Dale's super long dairy farm road. When he saw me getting pushed into the Escalade in handcuffs, he just shook his head in disappointment and gave me one of his looks.

27

First, I had no idea we had a U.S. Marshals office in Clover Creek and second, no idea what U.S. Marshals actually did. However, their building was super-secret in its location. Totally nondescript, the unmarked brick structure on the edge of town was near the furniture warehouse district. It easily blended into the background, like another warehouse or a small management building.

Marcus and I were separated, riding in two different cars and I hadn't seen him since we were summarily escorted from the dairy farm. I didn't see Wesley again either. I briefly overhead a discussion about jurisdiction before I was driven away. I was presently in a carpeted conference room with glass walls that looked into more conference rooms. It was basically a castle of conference rooms.

A short man with a cigar in his mouth and a huge belt buckle on his jeans clomped into the room. He introduced himself as Blaze.

"Is that your first or last name?" I asked.

"Think of me like Eminem or Pink. The name's Blaze. Just Blaze," he said, kicking his heels in for emphasis.

"Are those spurs on the back of your boots?" I asked. "And am I in trouble for speeding?"

"Yes, they're spurs and no, you're not in trouble for speeding. The U.S. Marshals Service does not patrol traffic," he said, unlocking my handcuffs. "Is that better?"

I instinctively massaged my wrists. "Much better. Does this mean I'm free to go because you already have the real killer, Juan Garcia, in custody?" I asked. I'd been waiting here for hours. The unidentified pick-up truck had to belong to Juan Garcia. Marcus confirmed that his SmartWatch GPS put him at the dairy farm as we pulled up.

He opened a file and started reading from it while pacing back and forth on the other side of the conference room table.

"Ava Decker, age twenty-seven. Graduate of Clover Creek High School in the town where she was born and lived all her life until she pursued an Accounting undergrad degree and a masters in Forensic Accounting from the University of California, San Diego. Passed the CPA on the first attempt and worked as a Forensic Auditor for almost a decade before moving back home to open a bakery. You were arrested multiple times for suspicion of various crimes but subsequently cleared of all charges. The locals describe you as a 'Nancy Drew with cupcakes,'" he finished, closing the file.

"The U.S. Marshal Service has a file on me?" I asked.

"No. We borrowed this from Officer Wesley Lockwood," he said. "And that's only page one of the file." He dropped a huge stack of papers in a manila folder on the table with a loud thud.

Wesley kept a file on me?

"What's the rest of the file say?" I asked as I reached for the manila folder, which he quickly pulled away.

"The rest of the file says you'd make an excellent U.S. Marshal," he said. "You meet all the qualifications and seem to have a knack for catching the bad guy, which is one of the most important things we do in the Marshals Service."

"What can I say? I have a special gift for always being in the wrong place at the wrong time," I said.

"Exactly. That's what we like to hear in the U.S. Marshals Service. Someone who seeks out danger and enjoys going where the bad guys are, putting their lives on the line in order to uphold justice," said Blaze, leaning over the table with both arms on it for support. "The pay level starts at a GS-07, which is over fifty thousand dollars a year, full benefits, 401K and two weeks of paid time off. What do you say?"

I looked behind me, to see if there was someone else in the room. Then I looked up at the cameras in all four corners. "Am I being punked right now? Did Wesley put you up to this to scare me into not investigating?"

"Nope. I'm recruiting you for the Clover Creek branch; I'm asking you to become a U.S. Marshal," he said, pointing to his badge, which was hitched onto his gun holster. It was shiny and silver. Without a phone to Google it for verification, it could've come out of a cereal box for all I knew about badges.

"Then what was up with the whole pointing a gun at me and hauling me here in handcuffs?" I asked. Didn't most headhunters try to attract you by wining and dining you, not frisking and arresting you?

"We were simply feeling you out. You handled yourself great, which only reinforces my opinion that you would make an excellent field agent," he said.

So basically, he wanted to see if I'd crack and start

crying like a big coward under pressure. Did he not notice in my file how many times I'd been arrested? Being marched away in handcuffs was like a new part-time hobby for me.

"Don't you need to be more athletic and fully adept in parkour in order to qualify for the U.S. Marshals Service?" I asked.

"That's what basic training is for. Five months of rigorous physical workouts in the hot, humid Georgia Savannah," he said.

Ha! As if. Although I did intend to add a little more exercise to my everyday routine, I was thinking more on the lines of a brisk twenty-minute walk with Lucky or maybe some light vacuuming around the house.

"Oh, yeah, that doesn't sound very appealing," I said. "I'm really busy baking cupcakes and taking care of my cat."

"I can whip you into shape in no time and the five months will fly by," he said, looking at me for a positive affirmation to which I shook my head *no* and made a big *X* with my forearms. "Well, you have another week to think about it. My offer still stands." He pulled out a business card from his front pocket and slid it across the table to me.

"So I'm not under arrest for the murder of Dale the Dairy Farmer or for stealing a one hundred thousand-dollar diamond engagement ring?" I asked, waiting for a camera crew to jump out any minute and yell *Psych!* or Wesley to suddenly come out laughing and say, *Gotcha!*

"Nope, again. Neither of those investigations fall under U.S. Marshals jurisdiction," he said.

"Then why was the U.S. Marshals Service there?" I asked. "Is Juan Garcia an international drug lord?"

"Nope, a third time. Look, sign this confidentiality agreement right here and then I can tell you everything you want to know," he said, pushing another manila file folder at me.

"Really?" I asked. Now, I knew this had to be a joke.

"Really," he said, pulling up a seat and leaning back before kicking his boots up on the table. He crossed his arms and looked from me to the manila folder in front of me. All right, I could play along. If he didn't want to break character, then I wouldn't either.

I opened it up and skimmed over the fifty-page document. It had a lot of legalese that obviously meant nothing since this was all some elaborately staged device orchestrated by Wesley. Since I knew he was only trying to teach me a lesson, I signed the bottom of the last page and pushed it across the table to Blaze. He took it and handed it off to another man who was waiting at the conference room doors.

"Juan Garcia is in the Witness Protection Program. Yes, he's a thief but not the kind you're thinking of. He's some sort of financial market hacker. He turned state's evidence against a group of international arms dealers who were using him to launder money and now he's in the Witness Protection Program. When the warrant for his arrest was issued, we moved in to relocate him again," he said.

I let out a loud laugh. When Blaze didn't respond, I cleared my throat and sat up straight.

"You're serious?" I asked.

"The U.S. Marshals Service is dead serious. Otherwise, people can get killed," he said.

"All right, can I speak to Juan Garcia?" I asked. If he intended to keep the charade up, then surely I would be allowed to speak to Juan after signing the extremely long legal document under the veil of secrecy.

"You can't. He's already been processed and is currently

en route to his new home and life," he said. "But what I can tell you is this: Juan briefly spoke to Dale the Dairy Farmer before he was killed. Dale believed the diamond thief was a super-rich old guy. He was doing deliveries with Dale that day and *he's* the one, not Dale, that saw a rich guy in a suit coming out of Frosted. Dale volunteered himself as the witness just to keep Juan off the police radar. Dale thought Juan was an illegal worker because Juan was moonlighting there for extra cash."

"Was the person he saw wearing a brown, old-timey-looking costume kind of suit?" I asked, already afraid of the answer.

He picked up another manila folder and looked through it. "Yes, I believe that's how he described it."

Ugh. I hoped my suspicions weren't true. "Am I free to go?" I asked.

"Itching to get out there so you can find the real culprit on your own?" he asked.

"Maybe. Why? Are you going to give me a big speech listing all the reasons I should stay out of this and go back to baking cupcakes?" I asked.

"Basic training starts next week and if you want to go around solving murders in your free time, then I would simply consider it more practice for a future career with the U.S. Marshals Service," he beamed, extending his arm out to the door.

Was now a good time to ask about their policy regarding emotional support cats on the job?

28

It was almost nine PM by the time the U.S. Marshals Service dropped me off at my bakery where the Aston Martin Valkyrie was parked out back. Caitlin had closed up long ago and Frosted was empty so all of the lights were off. I texted Shelby to ask if she could keep Lucky overnight. Then I texted Marcus who confirmed that the Marshals Service dropped him off at his house several hours ago. Now that I knew he was safe, it was time to get that missing diamond.

I gave a silent thank you to the universe when I noticed a light on over at Gorgeous Greens' back office area. I bolted in and beelined straight to the front where I heard Kira talking on the phone. I was about to walk in until I overheard her conversation.

"For the hundredth time, I don't care what your silly psychic powers tell you about the exchange rate for the Canadian dollar. Sell that stupid diamond engagement ring today, launder the cash at the casino on your way back and meet me at the flower shop in the morning," said Kira before slamming her phone down.

This was bad. Very, very bad. I hated being right, especially in this case. I thought about running away but I was mad, really mad. How could she do that to Tyler and Shelby? Why would she want to ruin their engagement when she wasn't even interested in Tyler anymore? And also, how could she do that to me? She knew how stressed I was about the robbery happening on my watch, in my bakery. All I'd ever done for Kira was help her. Not only with her sewing needs, but also covering her flower shop while she went out on auditions and supplying her with tons of free cupcakes and lattes. I felt like the world's biggest doormat friend right now.

Standing tall, I cleared my throat to get her attention. "How did you get the diamond out of the safe?"

At least, Kira had the decency to look startled. "What are you talking about?" she asked, searching the room for either an escape route or a weapon to kill me.

"Don't even bother. I recorded your entire conversation," I said, flashing my SmartWatch. I was totally bluffing but she didn't know that. "It's in the cloud and en route to Wesley right now."

She held her breath, still frantically searching for an escape hatch or possibly, a time machine. She finally let out a huge sigh and dropped into the chair in the corner with her head in her hands. "You have to understand. I didn't mean to hurt anyone. It was a victimless crime. Surely, you realize that. Even though you live in that big mansion and your boyfriend is a billionaire. I'm just so tired of always struggling," she said.

This was the third time I'd heard the victimless crime defense in the last week. Except this crime did have a victim: Dale.

"I'm pretty sure Dale would have to disagree," I said, moving closer to her at the cash register. Now that I finally hit the *record* button on the SmartWatch, I needed to hear Kira confess again. I also called Wesley as a backup and left the line open.

"He was going to blow everything. I offered to pay him off. I mean, how much can a dairy farmer make? I offered him half the cut from the sale of the diamond and he scoffed at me. He said the truth was more important than money. I didn't mean to kill him but the crossbow was hanging right in front of me. It's like Madame Omega always says: it was a sign from the universe," she explained.

I couldn't speak for the universe but I was positive that's not what it meant when she saw the crossbow at the farm. It was a good thing Caitlin took that anonymous summer scholarship or she might have been six feet under with Dale right now.

"Is that whom you were talking to on the phone?" I asked. Now it all made sense. That's how Madame Omega knew the ring would be stolen.

"Yes, she's an actress, too. I met her while auditioning at different productions around Blueberry Bay," she said.

"I knew it!" I practically screamed. She was such a fake. I couldn't wait to play this recording back to Shelby.

"But how did you get the diamond ring out of the box?" I asked. "I put that box in the cupcake myself and it was locked in the vault all day."

"That was easy. You were so distracted playing fetch with your cat, that I easily swiped it from the box after you'd already seen it. Once you sealed it up in that plastic baking wrap and threw it inside the vault, I knew I was in the clear," she said, inching her way toward the back door. "You even helped me sew it into the lining of my pants the first time. That's how I got it out of the bakery."

Ugh. It was official. I was not only the biggest doormat,

but also the biggest dunce for not noticing the ring in the pocket.

"How could you do this to me? I was your friend and you framed me for a diamond robbery!" I exclaimed, stomping after her. "And where do you think you're going?"

"Do you want me to pay you for sewing my costumes and all the free lattes and cupcakes? Because if you delete that recording, I should have all the money by tomorrow," she said, reaching into her toolbox. "In fact, I have a few thousand here I can give you now and more later. I know Frosted is on the brink of failure. Don't be like Dale. Just take the money."

"Or what? You'll kill me, too?" I asked, joining her on the other side of the room but keeping my distance one table away just in case. "I don't see any crossbows here."

She pulled out her garden shears and stalked towards me. "I'm also excellent at improv," she said.

"Stabbing me in the back isn't enough? You'd actually stab me to death?" I shouted, more annoyed than afraid at this point. I was five-foot-eleven with a good fifty pounds on her. All right, probably more than fifty. Kira was waif-skinny despite her wide hip complaining, which was why I always had to hem her costumes and alter her clothes.

Kira threw the shears at me, clipping me on the elbow. "Ow! That hurt," I snapped.

"It's not fair. You and Shelby get everything handed to you on a silver platter. I, on the other hand, have to work for everything I get," she said, picking up a potted cactus and hurling it towards my head, which I thankfully dodged. "You think it was easy finagling that stupid scholarship for your dumb baking assistant so I could get the lead role? No. It would've been so much easier to kill her but I didn't. I made her life better. And as for Shelby's ring. It would've been way easier to just kill her and steal the ring, but no. I went the extra mile to swipe it so that Tyler could file an insurance claim. That way, everyone wins."

Everyone, that is, but Dale.

Kira picked up the rest of her garden tools and threw them at me one-by-one. I hid behind a huge ficus tree until blood rolled down from my forehead. One of the spades she threw clipped me in the head. That wouldn't be pretty.

"You did this all for money?" I asked, jumping behind another plant but not before she dropped a half-open container of soil on me.

Nope.

Correction.

It was a half-open container of fertilizer.

Ugh.

The smell was already too much to bear.

"Not just for money. For fame. Every minute I waste taking care of this stupid flower shop is time I could be out there auditioning for bigger and better roles. I should be in blockbuster movies by now. Who knew Tyler could amount to something eventually? Someone who could afford a six-figure diamond engagement ring and ten expensive luxury sports cars? That ring and all of his money belong to me, not Shelby. I dated him first," she whined, pounding her fist on the table. "It's not fair."

She also dumped him first. Finders keepers. Wasn't that what Grant said about possession being nine-tenths or something to that effect?

"You could've sold the flower shop and moved to L.A.," I said. All this trouble was solely because Kira was too afraid to strike it out on her own.

"And then what? Hope I make it big in two tiny months because that's about how long the money from selling this dump would last. Unlike you, I rent this space. I wasn't as lucky as you to find a murdered boss like Francine who left me everything in her will," she said, hurling roses and glass vases at me.

"I wouldn't exactly call that lucky," I said, running behind the Japanese shrub garden.

"Oh, come on! In addition to your mansion and your bakery, you now own a three million-dollar sports car and you don't call that luck?" she said, picking up her signature pastel-colored tiny succulents and pummeling those towards me.

All right, from that perspective, I guessed I was pretty lucky. "All of those things still aren't worth killing someone for," I said. I would gladly give all of them back if Dale, Francine, and Tyler's sister were still alive.

"Well, we can't all have billionaire boyfriends to fall back on," she said, throwing her gardening overalls at me.

"He's not my boyfriend. We're just friends," I argued for the millionth time this week.

When Kira didn't answer, I looked up and saw that I was alone in the flower shop. Where did she go? I saw the front door closing and ran over. She dropped into the underground trolley construction area to escape.

Police sirens and blue lights were flashing on the street a couple seconds later. I pointed to the huge hole in the ground, blocked off by yellow caution construction tape.

"She's getting away!" I screamed.

Wesley did some sort of Parkour-looking move into the tunnel after her and resurfaced a few minutes later with Kira in handcuffs.

"Great job! That was amazing how you hurtled yourself into that hole without even looking to catch her," I said.

"I wasn't going after Kira. I was trying to get away from you. You smell terrible, Decker. You really gotta stop hanging out at that dairy farm so much," he said, waving the air in front of him.

29

After the EMTs checked me over, I headed to the police station to give my statement. Luckily. Grandpa Lockwood was there. He found some industrial strength soap and shampoo for me to wash off the fertilizer smell.

It only took a few minutes to relay everything back to Wesley and transfer the audio file to him, during which time his face went from its usual pale pallor to bright red. He reached over to his side drawer, popped two aspirins in his mouth and swallowed them without any water.

"Are you okay?" I asked, taking a seat next to him.

"Decker, I swear you'll be the untimely end of me," he said, pinching his nose while shaking his head back and forth.

"I'm pretty sure you mean, thank you for solving yet another one of your cases. You know, the U.S. Marshals Service was so impressed by my skills, they tried to recruit me," I said, leaning back and crossing my arms. "Despite all the bad things you wrote about me in my file."

"You, a U.S. Marshal? I don't think so. Look, I don't

have time for your jokes. I currently have a mountain of paperwork to comb through and the Canadian Mounted Police to coordinate with on arresting Madame Omega," he said, pointing to the mess on his desk.

"What's going to happen to Kira?" I asked while watching her get hauled away in cuffs to lockup in the back, a place I knew all too well.

"I'm writing up the arrest record now," he said, stopping his report. "And you're sure you don't want to press any charges?" He pointed to the bandages I sported on my elbows, forehead and shoulder.

"Oh, that? Those are nothing. Just some playful banter between gal pals," I said. Since Kira was in enough trouble already, pressing charges against her for assault seemed petty. Plus, I felt kind of sorry for her. I knew what it was like to have a dream but too afraid to go after it. That pretty much summed up the last ten years of my life as an accountant before finally inheriting Frosted.

"In that case, she's looking at ten years for the diamond heist and forty for second-degree murder charges," he said, tapping his ballpoint pen on his desk.

"Usually I'm happy about solving a case, but in this one, I'm just sad. Sad that Kira didn't have enough money or confidence to pursue her acting career full-time, sad that Dale had to die over a stupid ring, and mostly just sad that engagement rings seem to bring out the worst in people," I said, looking down at my ring-free, bare fingers.

"If you're referring to your ex's mother, I already took care of that for you," said Wesley, clicking through a few screens on his computer until a picture of the holding cell in the back showed up.

I leaned in closer and saw Evelyn, Ben's mother, looking extremely unhappy about being inside there. "No, you didn't?" I asked. "Is that even legal? Can you do that?"

"I can and I did. She's sitting on harassment charges," he said, leaning back in his chair and kicking his legs up on his desk.

"For what? I mean, she's extremely annoying but since when is being a horrible person against the law?" I asked. If it were, jails everywhere would be overcrowded.

"She did threaten you publicly on TV, thanks to Tessa. Free speech is no defense when it comes to threatening harm to someone," he said, crossing his arms and looking quite pleased with himself.

"Thanks, but I don't want you to be in her crosshairs; she can be pretty evil and overly vindictive," I said. I was super grateful but I didn't want anything bad to happen to Wesley. An angry woman with no job and excessive amounts of cash on hand who was obsessed with getting revenge? That couldn't be good for anyone.

"Bring it on. I'm not afraid. Besides, the only person allowed to harass and annoy you is me and I don't like competition," said Wesley with a smile.

30

"Wakey, wakey!" called out Ruby, snatching the comforter off my bed in one quick swoop.

I called Ruby to give me a ride home from the police station. She was a tad bit annoyed that I ignored her over the last few days but more than happy to be left out of the investigation.

We made up by doing one of our classic sleepovers of deep dish pizza and ice cream, after which I told her I could sleep in since Caitlin offered to open Frosted by herself for me in the morning.

So the next day, I was confused when the clock said seven AM and I found myself without any covers.

"Why?" was all I could groan as I looked longingly at the covers Ruby had flung onto the floor. I envied Lucky who was blissfully sleeping in with Skye at Shelby's place.

"So you don't want me to wake you up for Oreo Cookie and Double Chocolate Brownie Batter Pancake Towers at my parents' place?" she asked.

It was like hearing the voice of an angel when she said

those words. "Pancake Towers from Mr. Hardison? Ohmigosh, yes! I am so there."

Springing out of bed, I catapulted myself into the shower and was dressed and ready to go a few short minutes later. Construction for the underground train didn't start until eight AM so we got there without any problems this time. Just to be extra safe, we took Ruby's car instead of one of mine. Not that I had any worries about a three million-dollar sports car malfunctioning but historically whenever I got behind the wheel, our chances of successfully making it to our destination decreased significantly.

After we entered the front door, I kicked off my shoes and ran over to hug Ruby's father. "Mr. Hardison, you're my hero. You don't even know how sad it's been these last few days just thinking about the Pancake Towers we missed before."

He chuckled and hugged me back. "Don't worry, I'll always be available to make Pancake Towers for you girls," he said. "Which one do you like better, the Oreo Cookie or the Double Chocolate Brownie Batter?" he asked, mixing some batter in a bowl.

"Both," I answered.

Ruby pulled up a chair next to me after greeting her father and slid my phone towards me. "You left this in the car," she said. "It's been ringing off the hook like crazy. Don't you get alerts on your SmartWatch, too?"

"Yep, and I've been ignoring them," I said, sliding it back towards her. Nothing could come between me and my beloved Hardison Pancake Towers this time.

"Well, I answered it. It was Marcus. He said Madame Omega is getting away but he knows where she's at," she said, reaching her finger into the bowl and taking a lick.

"Ruby Hardison, mind your manners," said her dad,

playfully swatting her hand away when she went for another dip.

"I'm sure the police are all over it. Wesley can handle a harmless psychic," I said, jumping up to pour myself some freshly squeezed orange juice to go with my Pancake Tower.

"Wesley needs authorization from Portland law enforcement since it's out of his jurisdiction so he's in a holding pattern," said Ruby. "And hello, you could've poured me a glass of OJ." She got up and went to the fridge to retrieve the pitcher.

"Oh, right, sorry. I was so mesmerized by the pancakes, I completely forgot," I said.

Ruby's mother opened the back patio door and came bouncing in, fresh from her morning run. Not that you could tell since she didn't have a single bead of sweat on her. But I knew that was her morning routine because it was Ruby's, too.

"Well, good morning, girls," she said, giving us both a hug. "Who wants to go with me to Pilates?" she asked, reaching for her mat in the corner. This was the second part of her morning workout.

"Can't," I said, pointing to Mr. Hardison. "Pancake Towers."

"Well, you got me there. I can't compete with Pancake Towers," she said, grabbing her keys. "Please tell your parents hello when you see them this morning."

"My parents?" I repeated while feeling confused. They were still on their cruise.

"Yes, I just spoke to your mother last night. She said you promised to meet them in Portland when they returned so she could take you shopping for some knick-knacks to decorate the bakery," she said, tucking her mat under her arm so she could grab her purse.

"Yes, but that's not until the twentieth," I said, taking a sip of my OJ.

"Sweetie, today *is* the twentieth. I think their ship is docking right now," she said, looking at her watch and the calendar on the fridge for confirmation before nodding her head.

No! My precious Pancake Towers. This wasn't fair. Shouldn't I get some sort of medal for solving crimes or maybe even a day off?

Portland was a good two-hour drive, even in the Aston Martin Valkyrie. It was rush hour, which meant a lot of traffic on the road between Clover Creek and Portland. Thankfully, Marcus offered to take me in his helicopter so we were there in less than fifteen minutes.

"My parents are still disembarking," I said, once we started landing. "I bet we have time to track down Madame Omega."

Marcus gave me a thumbs-up.

Seeking out Madame Omega was really a moot point. Wesley confirmed that the local Portland police had already stationed themselves outside the cruise ship from Canada that Madame Omega came back on. They were simply waiting for Wesley's team to take custody of her so she could be processed back at Clover Creek. I was going for the sheer satisfaction of telling Madame Omega that it was I who figured it all out and that Shelby would no longer be needing her fake psychic services.

As we descended onto the docks, I was overwhelmed with all the cruise ships everywhere. My parents had taken my honeymoon cruise around the world and they loved it so much that they decided to sign up for another one. Their latest was an Alaskan cruise. However, I had never taken a cruise myself. This was all new and fascinating. There were lines upon lines everywhere we looked. Lines to get on the ships, lines to get off the ship, lines to enter the wharf, and lines to enter each cruise line company's waiting area. It was like a huge outdoor waiting room at a convention center.

"Whoa, how can we find anything in here?" I asked Marcus, who was already on it and swiping through his SmartWatch.

"This way," Marcus said, grabbing my hand and lacing his fingers through mine like we were on a date. I felt a small surge of warmth radiating from my palms straight to my heart. We weaved our way through the crowd, zipping in and out and between all the lines until we reached wharf block number seventy-four.

I saw Madame Omega in regular, everyday clothes, sans her Halloween costume. She was cuffed and under police supervision near the edge of the dock. I switched from following to leading and made my way over to her, more than ready to give her the verbal lashing of a lifetime for nearly ruining Shelby's love life in her selfish pursuit of money.

"Pumpkin, is that you?" asked my dad.

"Of course, that's her, sweetheart. She wanted to pick us up. And look, she brought her new boyfriend along with her for us to meet," said my mother, practically beaming as she looked from me to Marcus to our still clasped together hands.

"He's not my boyfriend," I said, disentangling myself from Marcus's hand. I sensed a surprised look from Marcus when I did that but it could've been caused by the unexpected run-in with my parents.

"Marcus, these are my parents, Forde and Kathryn Decker. Mom, Dad, this is my friend, Marcus." I emphasized the word *friend*, maybe a little too long but I didn't want to endure any more embarrassing moments.

"I think it's nice that you're taking care of our little Ava," my mother said, giving Marcus's shoulder a friendly pat.

"My little girl doesn't need a man to take care of her. She can take care of herself. Isn't that right, Ava?" said my father who was definitely the strongest feminist in the family.

"Yes, Dad," I said, glad he was here to intervene. I'd always been with Ben since I left home for college so my mother focused her energy on complaining that he wasn't the right guy for me. I had no idea she was so against me being single, which I found nothing wrong with.

Everyone exchanged hugs and handshakes before I realized Marcus was trapped for an entire day of knick-knack shopping with my parents. Since I had my own place, he had not yet been subjected to my mother's warehouse of trinkets and itty-bitty decorations, which identified the house I grew up in.

"Are we shopping all day or just a few hours?" I asked, wondering if I should just let Marcus return in his helicopter alone.

"We're not shopping at all. We heard there was another lead on Sakara's whereabouts and wanted to come back right away," said my mother. "Now, I don't want you to get your hopes up but it sounds promising; they've--"

"I know," I said, interrupting her.

"Is everything okay?" asked Marcus, sensing something was off. I gave him the small bit of details I had on my cousin, Sakara. She'd been missing since high school when she left for Georgia to look for her birth parents and we hadn't seen her since. To make the situation even worse, her parents also embarked on a search for her and now, they were also missing. In addition to amber alerts, my parents hired every private detective they could find but to no avail. It had been over a decade and after a pile of dead ends, we still had no idea what happened to Sakara or her parents.

"The anonymous donation to the Swiss Boarding School for the bakery was supposedly made by Sakara." I said. "But it could easily be another dead end." Or possibly someone playing a cruel joke by using her name on the donation but since it was anonymous, that seemed unlikely.

"I can help," said Marcus, already tapping away at his SmartWatch until I put my hand on his to stop him.

"Thanks, but we've been going down this rabbit hole for over a decade. Let's see if the police managed to discover anything worth digging into," I said. I was doubtful. Wesley offered to look into it two months ago and hit an impasse. I already felt bad that my parents had their hopes up again to simply come home and wait.

"Shall we go grab some breakfast together and get to know your friend a little better?" asked my mother, mocking me by emphasizing the word *friend* like I did earlier.

"Decker, what are you doing here?" asked Wesley, walking towards us.

"Picking up my parents from their cruise," I said, which technically wasn't a total lie.

"Oh," said Wesley, gulping down his entire Decker lecture on how I shouldn't intrude into police business. I introduced Wesley to my parents and did a silent groan when I saw the matchmaking wheels turning in my mother's head.

"Are you also a friend of Ava's?" asked my mother, emphasizing the word *friend* again.

Now it was my turn to drop my head into my hands and pinch my nose.

31

Two weeks later

"I can't believe you bought Shelby her own bookstore," I said, jumping up and down with excitement as Tyler and I stood in front of Gorgeous Greens.

"Me, neither. Having that ring stolen was the best thing that ever happened to us. Thanks for losing it," he said to me with a smile.

"Well, I wouldn't exactly call *Kira stealing it* as *me losing it* but sure, glad I could help," I said. I gave him a friendly pat on the shoulder.

Tyler and I scraped off the last of the Gorgeous Greens signage from the front window. While Shelby was at work, I'd been helping him to get the interior ready. We'd put a fresh coat of paint on all of the walls in Shelby's favorite color, a light lavender.

My mother was more than happy to apply her knick knack decorating skills to outfitting the entire place with complementary decorations, wall art, curtains and furniture. The dark mahogany bookshelves dotted the store. The walk-in flower case in the back was converted into a humidity controlled rare books room. And the best part of all was that we installed an open doorway so customers could travel back and forth between the two shops: Frosted and Shelby's new bookstore. But more importantly, so that Lucky and Skye and could hang out with each other all day together.

We covered the entire front window with a huge red ribbon to surprise Shelby with. My Palmer Tech Smart-Watch beeped. It was my ten minute warning.

"Are you sure you want me here?" I asked Tyler, not wanting to intrude on his new proposal to Shelby.

"Well, Shelby is already wearing the engagement ring I gave her back at her apartment last week so no chance of that disappearing again. And it's not like you can lose an entire store so we should be safe this time," he said, giving me a wink.

Tessa and her Channel Five news crew pulled up a few minutes later.

"Thank you for giving me the exclusive on this," said Tessa, giving me a hug like she hadn't totally tried to throw me under the bus earlier last week.

"Of course, you're my favorite reporter," I said.

"I am?" she asked.

Technically she was the only reporter I knew so sure. Why not?

"Definitely," I said.

"You know I only rigged that entire interview with Ben's mother to get her on public TV harassing and threatening you," she said.

"Really?" I asked. I wasn't sure if I believed that.

"It was Wesley's idea," she said. "How do you think he showed up so quickly to the bank? I don't think you coming out covered with purple dye was part of his plan but he meant well."

Wow. Wesley really was a good friend. I felt all warm inside hearing that story. Not the flushed warm that I got when Marcus was around but more of the inner happiness of knowing I had a big brother like figure looking after me.

"Thanks, Tessa," I said, giving her a hug. She didn't always go about things in the way I would but I appreciated that she had her own way of trying to be my friend.

A few minutes later, Shelby pulled up out front looking confused. She got out of her car and rushed over.

"Is everything okay?" she asked, looking from me to Tyler to Tessa. I knew it was killing her but Tessa didn't say a word and simply smiled in response.

Tyler took Shelby's hand and dropped to one knee. "Shelby Hicks, will you make me the happiest man in the world and go into business with me?"

Tyler threw his other arm out in a wide gesture towards the front of the store.

That was my cue. I ran over and untied the red ribbon holding up the brown paper covering the front store window to reveal the beautifully arranged bookstore interior.

"Ta da," I said, standing to the side so Shelby could get the full view.

"I don't understand," she said. "Go into business together?"

Tyler hopped up and opened the front door where Skye and Lucky were both waiting inside.

"I bought this for you. You've always wanted your own bookstore. Ava and her mother helped decorate it but you can do whatever you want with it or change it into a shoe store or a yoga studio," he said.

"Ohmigosh, Tyler. You did this all for me?" she asked, tears streaming down her face as Lucky crawled up her pants and into her arms. He squashed her tears with his paws. I had no idea where he'd learned that but that seemed to be his go-to response upon seeing tears.

"Yes, is it too much?" he asked. "I don't mean to be pushy and force you into anything. You can keep your job at the library and we can sell it if you don't want it. I only want you to be happy and you mentioned that you wanted to open your own bookstore someday and I thought why wait. Someday could be today."

I went over and retrieved Lucky from her. He happily jumped into my arms and started licking my face.

"No!" said Shelby. "I love it. And I love you."

Shelby ran over and hugged Tyler.

Hooray to that.

Tessa and her crew followed as we gave Shelby the grand tour of her new bookstore, including the hallway cutout to Frosted.

"This makes it even better. It's a bookstore with a cafe and bakery," she said. "And Skye and Lucky can be together all the time."

As if to confirm their approval, Lucky and Skye were rolling around, wrestling and playing with one of Lucky's red fuzzy balls on the Gorgeous Greens side.

"What are you going to call it?" I asked, excited about all the promotions and events we could do together.

"I'll have to make an appointment with Madame Omega at the prison later to go over potential names," she said, opening up the day planner she pulled out of her purse. "Kidding," she added before I had time to react.

I never got a chance to give Madame Omega the verbal smackdown I intended for her but I was on the slate to testify in court when her trial started next week and I didn't plan to hold anything back. The entire stolen ring debacle was worth it if it meant that Shelby finally felt confident enough to brave the world alone, sans a psychic.

"What about Diamond Books? We were just saying before you got here that if Ava hadn't lost your diamond engagement ring, then this might never have happened," said Tessa.

"Thanks for reminding us all of that, Tessa. What would we do without you?" I asked.

"Hmm. Diamond Books? I like it," said Shelby.

"Me, too," said Tyler.

"Plus, it'll make a great backstory," said Tessa.

32

The upside of having Wesley meet my parents was that they could no longer hint that he might be the one whenever I brought him up in phone conversations. Wesley made it clear that he already had a girlfriend. The downside of their newfound relationship was that they were now on Team Do-Not-Investigate-Crimes. Wesley not only became the world's biggest drama queen when emphasizing how dangerous it was, but he also ratted me out to my dad about not being able to pay the security camera service for Frosted.

"It looks even nicer than when we were here last time. Doesn't it, dear?" asked my mother, going around from table to table at Frosted, rearranging the new centerpieces that we swiped from Gorgeous Greens when Tyler bought it.

As much as I complained about my mother's knick-knack obsession, she was an excellent interior decorator. She helped me decorate the bakery with a large collection of violet petunias and pink impatiens that we hung around the display case. We also interspersed large, potted birds of paradise, olive trees and split leaf plants between the tables. On each individual table, she placed a large collection of pastel-colored succulents. It definitely perked the bakery up.

"And now that your security camera coverage is paid for the next year, no one can steal any of your plants," said my dad, taking another sip of his Vanilla Flat White. Gee, what a relief.

"I'm so glad Wesley told us about that. Really, Ava. What were you thinking? You should've called us if you needed money," said my mother, not trying at all to lower her voice. "And why are you suddenly investigating every crime that happens in Clover Creek?"

"Because she's smart and resourceful and once she sets her mind to something, she doesn't quit," said Blaze, coming in for his daily visit to Frosted.

"That's very well put. I don't suppose you're another friend of my daughter's?" asked my mother, emphasizing the word *friend* once again in that mocking way from when I first introduced Marcus and Wesley as only friends.

"I'm trying to be. The name's Blaze. I'd like to recruit your daughter for the U.S. Marshals Service," he said, tipping his ten-gallon hat at my mother as he introduced himself.

"You want my precious and only daughter to run around chasing dangerous fugitives?" asked my father, putting his drink down.

"You must be her dad," said Blaze, nodding towards him.

"Absolutely not. Ava's days of running around town endangering her life are over. Her mother and I are home now and we fully intend to put an end to that," said my dad, like I was still in high school.

I did a small eye roll when my dad put a protective arm around me.

"She's more than able to handle herself. Once we get her through five months of basic training out in the hot, humid Georgia Savannah, she'll be in fighting shape and ready for anything," said Blaze, making a bodybuilder arm pump pose that did not impress my father at all.

"Want your usual?" I asked Blaze, already heading behind the counter to make him a Mexican Mocha Latte. I handed him his latte and a cupcake to go.

"I'll be back again tomorrow to see if you changed your mind on joining the U.S. Marshals," said Blaze, heading out the door.

"She won't," said my dad, giving the front door an extra push for emphasis after Blaze exited.

"I could be a first-rate U.S. Marshal," I said to my dad.

My mother flashed me a picture of the weather app on her phone for Georgia. It was in the low hundreds all week with a heat advisory in effect.

She was right. Who was I kidding? I'd melt. And that was after I passed out from heat exhaustion. I specifically chose San Diego for college due to its temperate weather. Even the summers never went past the mid-eighties. I wouldn't make it one day in Georgia without being sheltered in constant central air conditioning.

"It would be a shame since you finally let me buy you that Brazilian Blowout," she said, running her fingers through my now straightened, sleek hair. It seemed excessively expensive at the time. I could've used that four hundred on a thousand other things but I had to admit, I loved it. No more crazy, out of control, fuzzy hair that looked like I stuck my finger in a light socket. For the first time ever, I could run an actual brush through my hair from top to bottom. It was supposed to last for at least two months but less than that if I were exposed to too much humidity. It would be back to stringy fuzz in under a week in Georgia.

"Mom, you have to stop petting my hair," I said, trying to shoo her off. She'd been obsessed with my new straight hair ever since the salon appointment. She was convinced that one of my new male friends would instantly fall in love with me at first sight and insisted that I go visit each of them.

"You inherited those out-of-control tresses from the Decker side of the family. All of the Barham women had beautiful, shiny, straight hair," said my mother, running her fingers through her own straight, brown hair.

"Yes, mother. You told me that before," I said.

33

I closed up Frosted at the end of the day and raced home to meet Marcus. He said he had something important to tell me.

My parents were officially back, which meant they commandeered both of their vehicles for everyday use. Luckily, I finally conquered the skill of driving a manual transmission. I easily pulled up to my driveway in the Aston Martin Valkyrie where Marcus was waiting for me in a dark red SUV.

"Is that a new car?" I asked as I crawled out of the Valkyrie. No one ever tells you how low to the ground Formula One race cars are. I had to get down on my hands and knees and bear crawl my way back to a standing position every time I exited the thing.

The opposite of graceful and dainty, that was me. On the plus side, simply getting in and out of the car was doing wonders for my ab muscles. Who needed the gym when you had an uber-expensive sports car to get in and out of on a daily basis?

"Yes, for you. It's the new Aston Martin DBX," said Marcus, tossing me the keys.

"You already bought me one car. And considering it was three million dollars, I'm pretty sure that covers you for life from having to ever do anything nice for me again," I said. Plus, this was how Tyler got in trouble with Grant in the first place: owning multiple cars.

"But I like doing things for you," he said, giving me a hug, which filled me with that same warm, squishy feeling. Why couldn't he kiss me and end all his mixed signals right there? All of these over-the-top gestures without any kissing were more than confusing. "And don't worry. I found a buyer for the Valkyrie. That is, if you're okay parting with it and only having this car?"

"Ohmigosh, yes. And I'm not taking a single penny from that car sale. It's all for you," I said. I didn't want to seem ungrateful but I felt super self-conscious with all the piercing looks I got from people in town when I drove it. This SUV was fancy looking but at least, it was only that, an SUV.

Lucky was excited to see Marcus and crawled up his legs until he was in his arms. Marcus gave him a friendly kiss and cuddled him. That proved he wasn't against kissing. He could kiss the cat.

Marcus walked over to the back of the SUV and popped the rear door open, revealing a doggy gate and a fluffy kitty bed inside. "I had it outfitted with their special pet package for Lucky."

Lucky wasted no time getting in, sniffing around and exploring the back.

"Wow, that's incredibly thoughtful of you," I said.

"Wanna take it out for a spin?" he asked, already closing the back door to secure Lucky in place.

"Definitely," I said, hopping into the driver's seat. "Are you thinking what I'm thinking?"

"Malnati's deep dish pizza for dinner?" he asked. "I've already programmed it into the GPS."

SNEAK PEEK OF CUPCAKES & CHAOS

The non-stop doorbell dinging and knocking on the front door woke me out of my peaceful slumber.

I slowly peeled myself off my mother's new aesthetically gorgeous but not-meant-to-be-slept-in couch that I'd fallen asleep on while watching yet another *Murder She Baked* movie marathon on the Hallmark Mystery Channel last night. I rolled my head from side to side, attempting to stretch the kinks out of my neck. The couch was so pretty, I thought for sure it would be more comfortable.

Oh, how I missed my beautiful, king-sized memory foam mattress and perfect ergonomic pillow back in San Diego with my luxurious six hundred thread count sheets.

I blinked my eyes open and held my hand up to block the light, trying to adjust to the bright morning sunlight. Taking a big inhale, I stood up, yawned and stretched myself awake.

The pounding at the front door was getting more intense. What was so urgent this early on a Saturday morning? My alarm hadn't even gone off.

And then I saw it.

The dead alarm clock. I hadn't been home in over ten years so I totally forgot the master light in the TV room was connected to the outlets on that side of the room. I must've killed the alarm clock when I turned off the lights.

I ran to the front door and threw it open, ready to tell whomever was there that I didn't have time to deal with them.

"I've been trying to call you all morning. Did you oversleep? You're late," said Ruby, stating the obvious.

Ruby, my best friend, was someone who never suffered from insomnia nor a bad hair day. Her thick chestnut locks cascaded around her perfect, heart-shaped face. She polished her look with a faux fur mauve scarf and matching hat and gloves.

"What time is it?" I asked.

"An hour past when you were supposed to be at the festival," she said. "Gwendolyn called my mother, who then called me, and I tried to call you. And now I'm here."

My previous adrenaline rush instantly morphed into electric bolts of panic. I brushed my teeth and got dressed at warp speed. I smoothed out my new baker's outfit, pristinely dry cleaned and smelling of lavender, and was about to put on my makeup before Ruby stopped me.

"Put it on in the car. I'll drive you to the festival," she said.

"Great idea but can you drive me to Frosted? Everything for today is already loaded in the Cupcake Delivery Truck that's parked in the alley out back behind the bakery. I need to drive that to the festival," I said, throwing my makeup bag into my purse. We both descended the stairs two at a time and I hopped into my Uggs as we ran out the door. We piled into her massively huge SUV, which I was just now realizing matched her scarf and hat. That was real commitment to a signature personal branding color.

I still had a small window of time before the contest registration started. If I were late to check in this morning, I could kiss my job at the bakery goodbye, which wasn't a big deal except it was the only bakery in town. Francine would surely fire me if I didn't make it there on the dot. Today's baking contest was being sponsored by the national publication, *Desserts, Inc.* magazine and the winner of today's bake-off contest was guaranteed a spot on next month's cover. That was all Francine kept talking about since I met her. She even spent all of yesterday at the spa getting herself picture perfect for her close-up.

Ruby drove me over to the alley behind Frosted in record time. I gave myself a mental high five for having the foresight to pack up the cupcake delivery truck last night before I closed up the shop. Everything I needed for today's bake-off contest was in the back. I triple checked it myself.

"I so owe you," I said, practically leaping out of Ruby's car before she even came to a complete stop.

"It's my job as the Watson to your Sherlock," she said, shooing me out of the car. "I'll find you at the festival later."

I only had ten minutes to get to a location that normally took twenty minutes without traffic. The festival was being held on the wharf, which was beautiful but not close to the Town Center where Frosted was located. Plus, parking would be a challenge at the festival in general and because I had no idea what the zoning rules were for setting up at the wharf.

Driving an oversized food truck was not for the faint of heart. I only had this job for a couple weeks now and I still wasn't used to driving such a behemoth vehicle. Normally a super slow, overly cautious driver, time was not on my side so I floored it and hoped for the best. Luckily, the roads were deserted.

For the first time ever, I saw red and blue lights in my rearview mirror.

Yes, I was going a few – all right, maybe a lot of miles – over the speed limit but in my defense, there was absolutely no one else on the highway and today was a make it or break it cupcake career day.

"Step out of the vehicle. Keep your hands where I can see them."

Yes, a speeding ticket really sucked but it was almost ten o'clock so if this went quickly, I could still make it in time. Everything went slower than normal in Clover Creek, including festival contest registrations. I gave a small plea to the universe that the cop pulling me over was a friend from high school or someone else I knew who would let me off with a firm warning.

I quickly jumped out of the gas-guzzling cupcake delivery truck, hoping for the quickest ticket delivery in history.

My reflection in the car window showed me holding my hands up, awaiting my fate. It wasn't particularly cold for a blustery winter morning in Clover Creek but at this angle, the wind flew straight up my shirt and chilled me like one of those deliciously cold scoops of ice cream that Claire, Frosted's biggest and only other dessert competitor, was probably doling out to contest voters right now at the bake-off.

The snow crunched under the cop's feet, getting louder as he came closer. I waited until he was right behind me before trying to plead my case.

"Officer, if you let me off with only a warning, I promise never to speed again," I said with the most sincere and helpless damsel-in-distress voice I could muster.

"That's original. Never heard that one before," he said in a way that indicated he was not at all interested in letting me off with just a verbal reproach.

A light breeze of patchouli wafted towards me as I turned around, catching me off guard. It smelled like I was on a date, a really hot date. Only men hoping to score wore aftershave or cologne that smelled like that. Or maybe it was me. Musky, sandalwood scents on men were my weakness.

I slowly looked up at the officer standing in front of me. Call me unimaginative but I expected to see a chubby, middle-aged cop when I turned around. Instead, standing in front of me was a cross between Adonis and Hercules. No way anyone could ever mistake this guy for an out of shape anything. Even though he was wearing the uniform, carrying the stick, and driving the car, he did not look at all like any cop I ever met. He was more like a stripper-for-hire heading to a bachelorette party. That he did resemble.

I waited a beat but he kept all of his clothes on. Not a stripper.

Even with his bulky winter coat, his broad, muscular delts came out loud and clear through the tapered V his shoulders created. His unbuttoned coat revealed a brawny, barrel chest leading to what I could only imagine were chis-eled abs of steel.

His badge read Officer Lockwood.

Like a crazy person, I immediately tested out my first name with Lockwood as my last name to see how it sounded: Ava Lockwood. I willed myself to stop staring but my eyes were on permanent surveillance. There was an electric current in the air pulling me closer. I inched towards him, unable to put the brakes on. Whatever he was selling, I was more than eager to buy.

He put his hands on his hips, right above his holster.

There was a small bandage sticking out from his side. I couldn't tell if it was a brace or a super large Band-Aid of some sort. He was going for intimidation but all I saw were washboard covered abs attached to a pair of sturdy, well-built legs. He was as close to an aesthetically perfect copy of the David statue as I've ever seen.

No wedding ring on the left hand: always a positive sign.

He bent over, putting his face where his waist was. "See something interesting?"

We might as well have been in the Caribbean for how hot my cheeks burned at that moment.

"I was wondering how you got that injury. Was it in the line of duty?" Jeez, that was lame.

A brief smile passed his lips, which meant he knew I was not looking at his bandage, nor admiring it in any way. He cleared his throat and resumed his tough guy demeanor.

"Bullet wound. Just a graze from last month's bank robbery," he said. "It's fine." He pulled his jacket further down to cover it up.

What was wrong with my brain? I swore off all men right after being left at the altar only a month ago. Did sleep deprivation make you boy-crazy?

Focus, Decker.

You need to get to the Bake-Off Contest. Soon. Very, very soon.

"You must be very brave and rise above wasting time on traffic control," I said, trying to appeal to his male ego.

He responded with a dead pan expression and completely ignored me. "License and registration."

I really had to work on my flirting skills. In my defense, I'd been dating Ben for the last ten years. The last time I flirted with anyone new was in high school and those were boys, not men.

I reached into the glovebox and my purse on the

passenger side and handed the items back to him with shaking hands, wondering how long this would take.

"Ava Decker," he said, reading my name off my license. "Want to tell me why you were going seventy in a fifty-mile-an-hour zone? What's the big hurry on a Saturday morning?"

"Yes, I'm really sorry about that," I said, pressing my hands to my chest to help demonstrate my deep desire to convince him to let me go. "I'm running late for the Delicious Desserts Bake-off contest down by the wharf this morning. Normally, I never exceed the speed limit."

Was it too early to ask again about getting a warning, preferably a verbal one?

"Wow. That's some sweet tooth you have," he said.

Great. Although, it wasn't entirely false. I could totally see myself doing that if the situation called for it. Like I did right after being left at the altar just a few weeks ago.

I started to point to the cupcake truck's signage to prove I wasn't just a sugar-addicted, crazed woman, racing through town from one sugar event to the next but the truck was a solid baby blue color. Francine's brother gave her this truck as a birthday gift last week so she could expand and sell her cupcakes in different areas of Blueberry Bay once the warmer summer months arrived. But since it was only February, getting a logo painted on the truck wasn't high on the winter priority list of tasks for the shop.

"I like sugar just as much as the next person but I'm not rushing there to eat. I'm one of the bake-off contestants, or I mean, I work for one of them," I said.

"You're a baker, huh?" he asked.

I could've sworn I saw a glint in his eye when I said that. It was the same look of excitement I had whenever anyone mentioned pastries, chocolate, ice cream or anything sugar-based. I found a fellow sweet tooth aficionado.

"Yes, would you like a sample?" I asked, hoping that would butter him up enough to let me go.

I motioned towards the back of the truck, which was filled with some of my special Chocolate Bourbon Pecan Pie and Bavarian Crème filled cupcakes for today's bake-off competition. No one could eat one of those and still want to give me a ticket.

"Is that a bribe?" he asked, raising an eyebrow and cracking the slightest beginning of a smile.

"Maybe we could call it evidence? Like, Exhibit A to prove that I really am a baker and totally running late to the world's most important baking contest of my life. Otherwise, I would have never and will never speed again in my life if you let me off with a verbal warning, kind of evidence?" I asked.

I walked towards the back of the truck.

"Stay right there, ma'am," he said, taking the keys from me. "I'll open the door."

Wow. Did he just ma'am me? I wasn't looking my best today but I was barely pushing thirty, not eighty.

In addition to making me boy-crazy, sleep deprivation also rendered me delusional because I could've sworn there was a spark between us earlier. Albeit, a small, possibly nano-level spark but definitely not a *Mrs. Robinson ma'am* type of situation! I was only twenty-nine and he couldn't have been much younger than that.

After he opened the door, I heard a sharp intake of breath.

Oh, no! Did all the cupcakes topple over in my crazy haste to get to the wharf? I had no idea how this monster vehicle operated under different driving conditions. There were a few potholes in the road on the way out here and the alley wasn't exactly smooth pavement central.

"Hands behind your head, interlace your fingers," he said, in a super serious, no longer flighty, flirty voice.

"What?" I asked, unable to think of anything more coherent or intelligent to say.

"You're under arrest," he said.

"Officer, this isn't what it looks like," I said, remembering Francine's crazy idea to bribe the judges with cash. She had a huge wad in a big package that she tried to pawn off on me the other day. I told her no but she must've snuck it into the back of the truck. A huge packet of cash looked weird to anyone.

"Right and I'm not really a cop. It just looks like I am," he said.

"But I can explain. That's not mine. It's my boss's," I said. "She put it in there last night."

"The dead body? That's hers?" he asked.

"What?" I demanded.

Did he just say dead body? Did sleep deprivation also jumble up words in your brain?

I peered around the corner and there she was: Francine Donovan with her beloved custom-made cake cutting knife plunged into her back. The word *Frosted* was engraved on the handle.

The air caught in my lungs. My heart immediately sunk into my chest and a cascade of tears streamed down my cheeks. Not that she was ever for a single moment nice to me but this was nothing less than horrible.

"Who would do such a thing?" I asked, silently sobbing my eyes out.

Until I felt a cold pair of metal rings being tightened around my wrists.

CUPCAKES & CHAOS is now available.

CLICK HERE to get your copy so that you can keep reading this series today!

STUFFED CUPCAKE RECIPES

Pumpkin Spiced Caramel Cupcakes With Cream Cheese Filling

Cupcake Ingredients

- 1⅓ cups all-purpose flour
- 4½ teaspoons espresso powder
- 1 teaspoon baking powder
- 1 teaspoon baking soda
- ½ teaspoon salt
- ½ teaspoon ground cinnamon
- Pinch of ground nutmeg
- Pinch of ground cloves
- ¾ cup canned pumpkin
- ½ cup granulated sugar
- ½ cup dark brown sugar
- ½ cup vegetable oil
- 2 eggs

Cream Cheese Filling Ingredients

- 8 ounces cream cheese
- ½ cup granulated sugar
- 1½ teaspoons vanilla extract
- 2 cups heavy cream

Homemade Salted Caramel Sauce Ingredients

- 1 cup unsalted butter, softened to room temperature
- 3 and 1/2 cups confectioners' sugar
- 1/2 cup (unsweetened natural or dutch-process cocoa powder
- 3 Tablespoons heavy cream or milk
- 1/4 teaspoon salt
- 2 teaspoons pure vanilla extract

Cream Cheese Filling Directions

1. On medium speed, beat the room temperature cream cheese, sugar and vanilla extract in a mixer with the whisk attachment until smooth and completely combined, about 3 minutes
2. Slowly add the heavy cream, scrape the sides of the bowl, then increase speed to medium-high and whip until stiff peaks form

Cupcake Directions

1. Preheat oven to 350 degrees F

2. Line a 12-cup muffin pan with paper liners
3. In a medium bowl, whisk together the flour, espresso powder, baking powder, baking soda, salt, cinnamon, nutmeg and cloves
4. In a large bowl, whisk together the pumpkin, both sugars and the vegetable oil until completely combined, making sure to break up any chunks of brown sugar so no lumps remain
5. Whisk in the eggs, one at a time. Add the flour mixture in two additions, folding with a rubber spatula until no flour pockets remain
6. Divide the batter between the baking cups, filling each about two-thirds full
7. Bake 18 to 22 minutes
8. Allow to cool in the pan for 5 to 10 minutes, then remove to a wire rack
9. Allow the cupcakes to cool completely before frosting before coring out the center and filling with cream cheese filling
10. Drizzle with homemade salted caramel sauce

Homemade Salted Caramel Sauce Directions

1. Add the sugar in an even layer over the bottom of a medium (3 to 4-quart) saucepan. Heat the sugar over medium heat, whisking it as it begins to melt. You'll see that the sugar will begin to form clumps, but that's okay. Just keep whisking and as it continues to cook, they will melt back down. Stop whisking once all of the sugar has melted, and swirl the pan occasionally while the sugar cooks.

2. Continue cooking until the sugar has reached a deep amber color. It should look almost a reddish-brown, and have a slight toasted aroma. This is the point where caramel can go from perfect to burnt in a matter of seconds, so keep a close eye.
3. As soon as the caramel reaches its sweet spot, add the butter all at once. Be careful, as the caramel will bubble up when the butter is added. Whisk the butter into the caramel until it is completely melted. Remove the pan from heat.
4. Slowly pour the cream into the caramel. Again, be careful because the mixture will once again bubble up ferociously.
5. Whisk until all of the cream has been incorporated and you have a smooth sauce. Add the salt and whisk to incorporate.
6. Set the sauce aside to cool for 10 to 15 minutes and then pour into your favorite glass jar and let cool to room temperature

Strawberry Filled Tiramisu Cupcakes With Mascarpone Buttercream Frosting

Cupcake Ingredients

- 2 cups cake flour
- 2 tsp baking powder
- 1/8 tsp baking soda
- 1/4 tsp salt
- 1-1/4 sticks (10 tbsp) unsalted butter, room temp

- 1 cup sugar
- 3 large eggs
- 1 large egg yolk
- 1-1/2 tsp vanilla extract
- 3/4 cup buttermilk

Espresso Extract Ingredients

- 2 tbsp instant espresso powder
- 2 tbsp boiling water

Espresso Syrup

- 1/2 cup water
- 1/3 cup sugar
- 1 tbsp Kahlua

Mascarpone Buttercream Frosting Ingredients

- 12 tbsp unsalted butter, room temp
- 8 oz mascarpone cheese, room temp
- 4 cups confectioners sugar, sifted
- 1 tsp vanilla
- 1 tbsp Kahlua

Strawberry Filling Ingredients

- 1/2 pound strawberries hulled and diced
- 2 tablespoons granulated sugar
- 1/2 tablespoon lemon juice
- 1/2 tablespoon cornstarch

Strawberry Filling Directions

1. In a saucepan over medium heat, add strawberries, sugar, lemon juice, and cornstarch
2. Bring to a boil. Reduce heat to medium-low and cook for 4-5 minutes, or until mixture has thickened
3. Set aside in fridge to cool while you prepare the cupcakes and frosting

Cupcake Directions

1. Preheat oven to 350F and line cupcake pan with liners
2. Beat butter until creamy
3. Add sugar
4. Add eggs one at a time, beating for about 1 minute after each addition
5. Add vanilla
6. Put flour mixture together in another bowl: Sift cake flour, baking powder, baking soda, and salt together in a separate bowl
7. Gradually add flour mixture and buttermilk, alternating each one into the bowl
8. Fill cupcake liners and bake for about 17-20 minutes or until a toothpick inserted in the middle comes out clean.
9. Remove from pan and cool completely on a wire cooling rack.

Espresso Extract Directions

1. In a small bowl, stir espresso powder and boiling water together until blended. Set aside

Mascarpone Buttercream Frosting Directions

1. Beat butter and mascarpone cheese until light and creamy
2. Add sugar and continue beating until smooth

Assembly Directions

1. Poke holes in cupcakes with a fork or toothpick
2. Spoon about 1-2 tsp of espresso syrup over each cupcake
3. Core out ½ inch from center and add strawberry filling
4. Using a large round tip pipe, frost each cupcake and sprinkle with cocoa powder

French Vanilla Cheesecake Filled Cupcakes

Cupcakes Ingredients

- 1 1/2 cups all-purpose flour
- 1 1/2 tsp baking powder
- 1/4 tsp salt
- 6 tbsp unsalted butter melted
- 3/4 cup sugar

- 1 egg plus 1 egg white, room temperature
- 2 tsp vanilla extract
- 1/3 cup milk
- 3 tbsp International Delight French Vanilla Coffee Creamer

Cheesecake Ingredients

- 1/2 cup heavy whipping cream
- 8 oz reduced-fat cream cheese 1 package - softened
- 1/4 cup sugar
- 1 tsp vanilla

Vanilla Frosting Ingredients

- 1 cup unsalted butter softened
- 4 1/2 cups powdered sugar
- 1 tsp vanilla extract
- 1 tbsp International Delight French Vanilla Fat Free and Sugar Free creamer

Cupcake Directions

1. Preheat oven to 350F
2. Line a muffin pan with cupcake liners and set aside
3. Whisk together flour, baking powder, and salt in small bowl and set aside
4. Cream together butter and sugar in a large mixing bowl until light and fluffy, about 3 minutes

5. Beat in the whole egg first, mixing until well combined, and then add the egg white, beating again.Add in the vanilla and beat until combined. Scrape down the bowl if necessary.
6. Add in half of the flour mixture and then the milk, beating until just combined.
7. Add in the remaining flour mixture and then creamer, beating until just combined.
8. Divide batter evenly among the cupcake liners. Bake for 19-22 minutes or until toothpick comes out clean. Let cool for at least one hour. Once cool, use a small knife or a corer to remove the center of the cupcakes.

Cheesecake Filling Directions

1. Whip heavy cream until stiff peaks form and store in fridge for one hour
2. Beat cream cheese until light and fluff
3. Beat in sugar and vanilla and continue beating until well combined
4. Fold in whipped cream
5. Transfer cheesecake mixture into a large ziploc bag. Cut off one bottom corner of the bag and use the bag to pipe the filling into the cheesecakes. You will have some leftover.

Vanilla Frosting Directions

1. Beat butter for several minutes until nice and creamy
2. Gradually beat in the powdered sugar, then the vanilla extract and creamer

3. If the frosting is too thick, add additional creamer 1 tsp at a time or if too thin, add powdered sugar 1/4 cup a time
4. Pipe frosting onto cupcakes and top with sprinkles

MORE LISA!

ABOUT LISA SIEFERT

Lisa Siefert is a huge fan of cupcakes and carbs, a planner girlboss and author of the new Frosted Misfortunes Mystery series. She is a devoted fan of all things chick-lit and rom-com and dedicates all of her free time to testing out new latte flavors at every coffee shop she comes across. She lives in San Diego with Lucky, her own devious Abyssinian kitten. She can also whip up a mean mint chocolate chip ice cream batch.

MORE BOOKS LIKE THIS

Welcome to Whiskered Mysteries, where each and every one of our charming cozies comes with a furry sidekick... or several! Around here, you'll find we're all about crafting the ultimate reading experience. Whether that means laugh-out-loud antics, jaw-dropping magical exploits, or whimsical journeys through small seaside towns, you decide.

So go on and settle into your favorite comfy chair and grab one of our *paw*some cozy mysteries to kick off your next great reading adventure!

Visit our website to browse our books and meet our authors, to jump into our discussion group, or to join our newsletter. See you there!

www.WhiskeredMysteries.com

WHISKMYS (WĬSK'MƏS)

DEFINITION : a state of fiction-induced euphoria that commonly occurs in those who read books published by the small press, Whiskered Mysteries.

USAGE: Every day is Whiskmys when you have great books to read!

Made in the USA
Monee, IL
30 November 2021

83527696R00132